"Are you te_____y's in trouble?

"No," Alex repli__ ___ _____ _____ __ ____ called Tantilla could get into trouble. And the U.S. could be in danger if Tantilla were ever overthrown. The president of Tantilla's daughter and her husband came to the U.S. on a diplomatic mission. They've been in D.C. for a week, and they were supposed to spend a week in Houston, but they've disappeared."

Mel's eyes got bigger.

"I'm told they do this all the time. It seems they're newlyweds who can't keep their hands off each other. They'll be found within a few days at most. In the meantime, it's in everybody's best interest that the U.S. keeps it completely secret that they are missing."

She blinked at him. "How the hell do they plan to do that? Someone's going to impersonate them?"

Alex stared her into her eyes. "Not someone. *Us.*"

Dear Reader,

As the year winds to a close, I hope you'll let Silhouette Intimate Moments bring some excitement to your holiday season. You certainly won't want to miss the latest of THE OKLAHOMA ALL-GIRL BRANDS, Maggie Shayne's *Secrets and Lies*. Think it would be fun to be queen for a day? Not for Melusine Brand, who has to impersonate a missing "princess" and evade a pack of trained killers, all the while pretending to be passionately married to the one man she can't stand—and can't help loving.

Join Justine Davis for the finale of our ROMANCING THE CROWN continuity, *The Prince's Wedding*, as the heir to the Montebellan throne takes a cowgirl—and their baby—home to meet the royal family. You'll also want to read the latest entries in two ongoing miniseries: Marie Ferrarella's *Undercover M.D.*, part of THE BACHELORS OF BLAIR MEMORIAL, and Sara Orwig's *One Tough Cowboy*, which brings STALLION PASS over from Silhouette Desire. We've also got two dynamite stand-alones: Lyn Stone's *In Harm's Way* and Jill Shalvis's *Serving Up Trouble*. In other words, you'll want all six of this month's offerings—and you'll also want to come back next month, when Silhouette Intimate Moments continues the tradition of providing you with six of the best and most exciting contemporary romances money can buy.

Happy holidays!

Leslie J. Wainger
Executive Senior Editor

Please address questions and book requests to:
Silhouette Reader Service
U.S.: 3010 Walden Ave., P.O. Box 1325, Buffalo, NY 14269
Canadian: P.O. Box 609, Fort Erie, Ont. L2A 5X3

Maggie Shayne
SECRETS AND LIES

INTIMATE MOMENTS™

Published by Silhouette Books

America's Publisher of Contemporary Romance

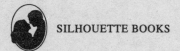 SILHOUETTE BOOKS

ISBN 0-373-27259-6

SECRETS AND LIES

Copyright © 2002 by Margaret Benson

This edition published by arrangement with Harlequin Books S.A.

® and TM are trademarks of Harlequin Books S.A., used under license. Trademarks indicated with ® are registered in the United States Patent and Trademark Office, the Canadian Trade Marks Office and in other countries.

Visit Silhouette at www.eHarlequin.com

Printed in U.S.A.

Books by Maggie Shayne

MAGGIE SHAYNE,

a *USA TODAY* bestselling author whom *Romantic Times* calls "brilliantly inventive," has written more than twenty-five novels for Silhouette. She has won numerous awards, including two *Romantic Times* magazine Career Achievement Awards. A four-time finalist for the Romance Writers of America's prestigious RITA® Award, Maggie also writes mainstream contemporary fantasy, as well as story lines for network daytime soap operas.

She lives in rural Otselic, New York, with her husband, Rick, with whom she shares five beautiful daughters, two English bulldogs and two grandchildren.

Chapter 1

"Look, it's not going to be all that tough for you to impersonate Thomas Barde. He's only important by marriage, and he's rarely seen publicly. Especially here in the U.S." The man Alex Stone trusted most in the world, Mick Flyte, took a pause to rub his chin thoughtfully. "The tough part is going to be finding a woman who can impersonate *her*. Everyone knows what Princess Katerina looks like."

Alex leaned back in his comfortable ergonomic chair, looking at the men who sat around the long, narrow table. "Everyone but me, I guess. Until just now, I'd never even heard of any island nation called Tortilla."

"Tantilla, Alex," Flyte said with a scowl. "And she's not a princess, in truth. She's the first daughter. 'Princess Katerina' is just what the people have nicknamed her. They adore the girl."

"Whatever. Look, I'm not working for the government anymore. Didn't you guys hear? I'm an independent now.''

''That's why we need you to do this, Alex. It's important. It's vital. And it's not gonna be that big a challenge.''

The second voice belonged to one of Alex's best friends, Caleb Montgomery. He'd been called to Tulsa from Big Falls, Oklahoma, for this meeting. Apparently the powers-that-be thought he could help convince Alex to go along with this harebrained scheme. Some of the most well-known political figures in the nation, most of them retired now, were gathered in this conference room within the heart of the Federal Building on a Sunday, when it should have been closed. The doors were guarded by armed soldiers. Mick Flyte had been Alex's superior during his Secret Service days. Caleb was the son of one of Oklahoma's former U.S. senators and a powerful attorney in his own right, though he spent most of his time in his small-town office since settling down with that Brand girl, Maya.

That thought led to another—of Maya's hellcat sister, Mel. He'd thought of her several times since his recent visit to Big Falls, each time with a shiver of dread at the thought of ever having to see the woman again. She was crude, tactless, violent and she had a mouth on her like a sailor. He suppressed a shudder as her face flashed through his mind. Tiny and elfin, capped in short jet-black hair, and deceptively innocent. Those jewel-blue, almond-shaped eyes sparkled with trouble and hellfire.

''Alex?''

He shook away his thoughts, glanced at Caleb and nodded as if he'd been listening the entire time. ''Look, I'll listen to your pitch, okay? That's all I can promise.''

There was a sigh of relief among the men in the room. One gave a nod to another, who dimmed the lights and flicked on a slide projector. Alex rolled his eyes, feeling as if he had fallen into a scene from *Mission Impossible*. Good God, could they get any more cloak-and-dagger?

A tall, slender, nice-looking man in a very expensive suit filled the screen. He wore sunglasses and a full beard. "This is Thomas Antony Barde," Mick Flyte said. "He married President Belisle's daughter, Katerina, six months ago in a secret wedding designed to keep the press away. It worked. I've never seen him in public without the glasses and beard."

"His height and build look about right," Caleb volunteered, glancing from the image on the screen to Alex and back again.

"Yeah, yeah. Let's cut to the chase, shall we? Why is it you want me to impersonate him?"

The men all sighed. It was Caleb's aging father, Cain, retired U.S. senator, who rose and spoke. "Thomas and Katerina are guests of the U.S. They came as representatives of Tantilla, because President Belisle was unable to make it himself. This has been set up for months. All pomp and ceremony, really. Tantilla is small, and its government none too stable. They want U.S. aid."

"And what's in it for us?" Alex asked. When the men frowned at him, he only smiled. "Oh, come on, there's always something. We don't give aid to just anyone."

Mick Flyte cleared his throat. "Tantilla is sitting on a veritable ocean of crude oil, most of it still untapped."

Alex nodded slowly. "So the little princess and her new hubby come tour the U.S., get a few photo ops, make nice with the White House, and...?"

"And spend a week in Austin as guests of the governor of Texas. Barde was supposed to meet with some of our leading oilmen there, get advice and input on future drilling and so on," Cain Montgomery said.

Alex listened, tried to get to the truth beneath the words. "*Was* supposed to meet with them? Has something happened to prevent it?"

"Uh…well, we're not sure," Flyte said.

"What's that supposed to mean?"

Mick Flyte cleared his throat. "The couple arrived in Austin from D.C. as scheduled, and were taken by limousine to the house where they were to be spending a week as guests of the state. But shortly after arriving at the house, they, uh, well, they vanished."

"Vanished?"

Flyte nodded.

"Did someone get to them?" Alex asked, alarmed. "Does this government have enemies out to—"

"All governments have enemies, Alex, but that's not what happened. These two are…well, they're notorious for this kind of thing," Flyte explained.

"What kind of thing?"

Caleb cleared his throat. "They're still newlyweds. They seem to be madly in love with each other, and they have a habit of taking off without warning anyone, shaking their security teams and going off on some romantic lark, just the two of them."

Alex frowned. "Isn't that kind of stupid of them?"

Caleb shrugged. "You do stupid things when you're in love. But, it's not exactly safe for them, considering who they are. They always turn up in a couple of days. Either their security team finds them holed up in a love nest somewhere or they come back on their own."

"So, then, what's the big deal?" Alex asked.

''The big deal is that we don't want anyone to know they were ever gone. President Belisle trusted us with the safety and security of his only daughter. It would look very bad for us to admit we lost her,'' Cain Montgomery explained. ''We have the FBI and the CIA on this. We have no doubt we'll locate the couple within forty-eight hours at the most, and once we know they're safe and sound, things can continue as planned.''

''That's not the only reason. Come on, Dad, he deserves the truth,'' Caleb said.

Sighing, Cain went on. ''Tantilla does have enemies. Small groups, unorganized for the most part. Still, they're likely paying close attention to this visit. We feel that if it became public knowledge that Katerina and her husband were missing, those groups might attempt to find them before we do.''

Alex nodded. ''So the plan is…?''

''The plan is to go ahead just as if everything is normal. Put a couple in place to impersonate them at various functions, buy us the time we need to find the real couple and get them back here,'' Mick Flyte said. ''Meanwhile, all you need to do is pose as Thomas Barde, attend a few dinners and social events, and basically be treated like royalty for a few days, all on Uncle Sam's nickel.''

''Yeah, but aren't you forgetting one very important factor in all this?'' Alex asked. ''You have to find a woman who looks and acts enough like this Katerina Barde to fool the who's who of U.S. political and social circles. That's not gonna be easy. Do we even have an agent who resembles her?''

''Finding the woman to play the role is next on our list,'' Caleb said. ''I don't know what the princess looks like, either. Guess I've been living out of the loop for too long." He gave the man at the slide projector a nod. "You have a photo?"

The man nodded back and clicked his controller.

The face that filled the screen was the same one that had been invading Alexander Stone's dreams ever since he'd helped save her sister from a crazed stalker a year ago. Melusine Brand. The roughest, crudest, toughest, mouthiest, most self-confident woman he'd ever met in his life.

He had never seen her, however, wearing the sweet, demure expression of the woman on the screen. Nor had he seen her wearing makeup like that, or clothes like those, or with gentle curls in her raven hair.

Alex swallowed hard and glanced at Caleb with an unspoken question.

Caleb was shaking his head. "No. No way you're dragging my sister-in-law into this. My wife would freaking kill me. My mother-in-law would string me up. No. We can't ask Mel."

"Oh, but we *can* ask Alex, right, pal?" Alex said with a slap on his friend's shoulder. "Guess I know where I stand in your food chain."

"She's *family,* Alex."

Alex sighed, then glanced at the others. "Is there any danger at all in this?"

"Absolutely not," Mick Flyte said.

"None whatsoever," Cain agreed. "No one even knows they're missing. As far as the Secret Service men assigned, they've been hand chosen. None of them were men you worked with, Alex. None of them know you. As far as they're concerned, you're the real deal. They'll be protecting you as such."

Pursing his lips, Alex nodded. "Then you have to ask her." He glanced at Caleb.

"She'll refuse. She'll flat-out refuse. And if she accepts, her mother won't let her do it, anyway."

"Oh, I can talk to Vidalia," Cain said. "I think we can get past all that."

"Maybe," Alex said. "If you do, that's only the first leg of the battle, though. Because Mel Brand may look like a princess, but that woman is the furthest thing from one." He glanced at Cain. "Can you afford to hire the entire staff of the world's most successful charm school?"

"Does all this interest in our plan mean you're in, Alex?" Flyte asked.

He drew a deep breath. "Look, I don't like politics. That's why I left. But I can probably find you someone else."

"It pays more than you'll make in five years," Cain said.

Caleb shook his head. "Alex doesn't give a damn about money. He has plenty of his own, and his principles are more valuable to him."

"Thank you for that."

Cain spoke again. "Melusine Brand cares about money. Hell, it's more than she has ever even imagined earning. And we're gonna ask her either way."

Alex frowned.

Caleb snapped his gaze to his father. "You knew Mel looked just like this princess before we ever got here, didn't you?"

His father nodded. "Tantilla is a tiny nation, son. But it's one with oil out the wazoo and nuclear capability. This is more important than just finding a pair of wayward lovers. We need ties to this government. We need to keep it in power. Its enemies, though small and unorganized, are a real threat, and just radical enough to use weapons of mass destruction against perceived enemies, which would include most of Western civilization. I think once Mel knows that, she'll agree to do her part to protect the world.''

Caleb licked his lips, glanced at Alex. ''He's right. She will.''

''I know she will, the stubborn, scrappy little harridan.'' He sighed. ''But she'll blow it if she tries.''

''Unless you're there to help her. It's only three days at the most, Alex.''

''A minute ago you said forty-eight hours.''

''In all likelihood, that's all it will be.''

Alex sighed, lowered his head.

Caleb came around the table and put his hand on Alex's shoulder. ''You're my friend. If I have to see my wife's sister dragged into this, Alex, it would mean a lot to me to know you'll cover her back.'' He paused. ''I'd do it for you.''

Pursing his lips, Alex lifted his head and looked Caleb in the eye. ''Hell, I don't know another man who could stand her for three days. All right. I'll do it.''

The saloon was packed, and Melusine Brand was winding her way between customers with a tray full of frosted foamy mugs held over her head, when a big, male hand cupped her left buttock.

She stopped in her tracks, turned her head slowly and met the soused cowboy's unfocused eyes and crooked smile. ''Like the song says, Brett, 'What part of *no* don't you understand?' ''

''Ah, honey, you know I'm not the kind to take no for an answer.''

''Well, hell, then I guess I may as well surrender.''

She smiled at him, blinking her eyes rapidly. "You want to take me outta here, hon? Someplace...private?"

"Whoo-boy. I surely do."

"I thought so, being that you've grabbed my ass three times now."

"I knew you liked it."

"Yeah, that's why I kept telling you stop. You just hold this big ol' tray for me, hon. I'll shuck this apron, and we'll get outta here." She lowered the tray, and people made room for her. Brett took it from her, grinning, and she unknotted the white apron and peeled it over her head. "There. You ready?"

"Yeah. Uh, what about the tray?"

"Oh, silly old me. I guess we'd better get rid of these drinks, huh?"

Someone muttered, "Oh, crap, here we go again."

Mel picked up two of the mugs, brimming full of icy cold beer, and poured them over Brett's head. He scrunched his face up, spat and sputtered, turned red and let go of the tray all at once. The tray hit the floor, and the remaining mugs clattered, cracked, and shattered. Beer washed over the floor.

"Oh, now, Brett, you shouldn't've gone and done that. Look at the mess you made."

"Damn you, woman!" He took one long stride toward her, over the mess on the floor. By now the crowd had parted to give them plenty of room. Brett reached for Mel, but she still had the two empty mugs in her hand, and she brought them together, hard and fast, on either side of his head. Then she kneed him in the groin for good measure. He doubled over, so she brought an elbow down onto the back of his head, and he landed facedown in the spreading pool of beer.

The crowd burst out with hoots and hollers. Brett

started to rise, but Mel planted a foot on the small of his back to keep him down. "Now listen up, Brett. When a woman tells you to stop groping her, that means she wants you to stop groping her. You understand?"

He pushed himself up. She pushed him back down. "Do you understand?"

"Yes!"

"Good. Now get up, and get out. You're banned for a month. And when you come back, you damn well better have learned some manners."

She removed her foot. He got up on all fours, then rose slowly to his feet, wiping beer from his hair and face. "Damn you to hell, Melusine Brand," he muttered.

"You watch your mouth, young man," Vidalia Brand called from behind the bar. She held a baseball bat in a fierce grip. "Now git, like my daughter told you, before I come over there and take a turn."

"All right, I'm goin'!" He hurried out the door, suddenly more sober than he'd been before.

Mel brushed her hands against each other and bent to pick up the fallen tray. Her sister Kara came from behind the bar with a mop, and the patrons returned to their conversations as if nothing all that unusual had happened.

Probably, Alex figured, because it hadn't. He'd had a perfectly unobstructed view of the entire event, being at a small round table two feet from where Mel was bending over right now. Getting her for this job was a huge mistake. He didn't like her. She would never fit into society, which was just as well, because she wouldn't want to. She considered men like him to be useless pretty boys, all manners and no guts. She'd as much as told him so the last time he'd encountered her.

Still, for the good of his country, Alex got to his feet, walked over to her and cleared his throat. "Can I give you hand with that?"

She straightened, not turning. Kara looked up, too, and smiled at him so warmly that he found it kind of touching.

Mel said, "Is that a *GQ* P.I. standing behind me?"

Kara nodded, and Mel turned to face him. She was a head shorter, so she had to tip her face up to look at him. "Well, I'll be damned. What is the slickest city slicker I've ever met doin' back down here in hicksville?"

"Came to see you, Mel. I hadn't been insulted in so long I was having withdrawal symptoms."

"You shouldn't be mean, Mel," Kara said, shouldering past her shorter sister. "Alex helped save my life, and Edie's, too." She reached out and gave Alex a timid hug. He hugged her back just a little. "How are you, Alex?"

"Just fine, Kara. And you?"

She shrugged. "I'm mostly over it. I still get nightmares every once in a while, though." She started toward the bar, taking his hand and tugging him with her. "Selene, Mom, look who's here!"

Vidalia smiled and waved a welcome. Selene, the youngest sister, narrowed her eyes on him, then slid her knowing gaze to Mel. "I told you he'd be back," she said.

"What'll you have, Alex?" Vidalia asked. "And keep your wallet in your pants, son, your money's no good here."

"I'd like to talk with Mel, if I could."

"Oh?" Vidalia blinked and looked past him at Mel, who was finishing the cleanup and making her way to the bar with the trayful of broken beer mugs in one hand and the beer-soaked mop in the other. "Well, I guess I can spare her for a while."

"Spare who?" Mel asked.

"You, hon. Alex, here, wants to talk to you for a while. That okay with you?"

Mel glanced at Alex, her eyebrows raised. "What do you want?"

"Just what she said. To talk to you. Privately, if we could."

"About what?"

He would never get used to her direct, in-your-face mannerisms. "About a job offer."

"For me?"

"Yes. For you."

Her dark brows pulled closer. "What kind of job offer?"

"One that pays a million dollars for three days' work," he said finally.

That shut her up. She blinked in shock, looking from him to her mother, then to each of her sisters in turn.

"So will you come with me so we can talk, or shall I go find somebody else?"

"I'm coming. Sheesh, are you on a time limit or something?"

"Yes, and there's not much of it." He took the mop from her and leaned it against the bar then reached for the tray, handing it over the counter to her mother. "Mrs. Brand—"

"Vidalia to you, son."

He smiled at her. He couldn't help it, he liked the woman. Which was kind of odd, because she was an older version of her rowdiest daughter, and he couldn't stand the latter. "Vidalia, if it's all right with you, we'll meet you back at your house right after closing time. This discussion involves you, too.''

"All right. I'll close up a mite early and put on some coffee and brownies.''

"Sounds great.'' He glanced at Mel. "You ready?''

"Sure. Are you?''

He closed his eyes briefly. "I doubt it. Come on.'' He led her to the door.

Mel would never in a gazillion years admit to this city-bred, spit-polished, overly educated male model that she had been unable to breathe when she'd first heard his voice. It wasn't that she *liked* him. In fact, she actively *dis*liked him. He was a glorified P.I., and that was all. Just because he called his business a "private security firm,'' and just because he was an ex-Secret Service agent, and just because all his clients were richer than God and almost as famous, didn't change a thing. He was a P.I. A gumshoe. A dick.

According to Caleb, the guy's services were in such demand that he could afford to name his price, handpick his clients, and work only when he wanted to. Mel silently bet that was mostly because he had the looks and manners of Prince Freaking Charming.

He opened the doors of the saloon for her and took her elbow, just lightly in the palm of his hand, when she walked down the steps to the waiting car. A Mercedes. Of course it was a Mercedes. He opened the door for her and held her arm until she was safely in. Then he closed it gently and went around to his side. Then he started the car, fastened his seat belt, reached out to adjust the heat.

She noticed his hands then. They'd caught her attention before, and she found them just as interesting now.

Long and narrow. They moved gracefully. It wasn't an effeminate quality; it was very masculine, in fact, but different.

It did something to her belly to watch him move his hands.

"So where shall we go?" he asked.

She shrugged. "This is your project, Alex. I don't even know what it's about." But her brain was replaying his earlier words. A million dollars for three days' work. "Do I have to kill someone?"

He was backing out of the parking lot, but the question made him stop in the middle of the road and send her a probing look. "*Would* you?"

She shrugged. "No. Not for money."

"No?" He put the car into drive, straightened it out and started down the road. "What would you kill for, then?"

She glanced sideways at him. "What do you think? That guy who had my sister strung up in that barn last year? I'd have killed him in a heartbeat."

He nodded. "So you'd kill to protect your family."

"Wouldn't you?"

He didn't answer, just kept driving.

"Now you've got me curious," she said. She thought about his job as a Secret Service agent. That would imply being willing to kill to protect his employer. Or die to do the same. Wow. What kind of man did it take to do something like that? Had he ever killed anyone? she wondered, staring at his profile. He glanced at her. She looked away. "Turn here, we'll go up by the Falls."

He turned the car up the dirt road and drove slowly over the potholes.

"So why all this talk about killing?" she asked. "Is that really what this job is about?"

"No, of course not."

"Right there, that turnoff."

He squinted. "Is that a road?"

"Yeah, just a short one. Leads to the Falls." He turned, and they rolled forward. He stopped the car. The road ended at the edge of a wide chasm, and on the opposite face, the powerful Falls tumbled down from a dozen yards above, plummeting into the river, far, far below.

"I didn't get to see this the last time I was here," he said. He pulled on the emergency brake, opened the car door, got out. He started toward her side, but she was out long before he got there.

"Beautiful, isn't it?"

"To say the least."

"This is where your buddy Caleb knocked up my sister, you know." She glanced at him in time to see him wince, closing his eyes tightly and sucking air through his teeth. "What?" she asked.

Sighing, he looked at her. "This is where the twins were conceived."

"That's what I just said."

"No, you said it was where Caleb knocked up your sister. There's a difference. Try it my way."

She rolled her eyes. "What is this? Are you on some kind of 'Enry 'Iggins trip, or what?"

"In a way I guess I am. Now try it. This is where the twins were conceived."

"This is where the twins were conceived...."

"Very good."

"When your best friend knocked up my sister."

He tipped his head back and stared up at the stars as if seeking help.

"So c'mon, tell me about this job. What in the world could I possibly do in three days that would be worth a million bucks to anyone?"

He brought his eyes level with hers. "Save the world."

She threw her head back and laughed out loud. But when she looked at him again, he wasn't even smiling. Her laughter died. "Oh, come on," she said. "Cut it out. You just wanted to see me again, right? So you concocted this scam and..." He was shaking his head slowly, left then right. "Are you telling me my country's in trouble?"

"No. A tiny little country called Tantilla could get into trouble. And the U.S. could be in danger if Tantilla were ever overthrown."

"Why?" she breathed.

"I can't tell you that."

She blinked at him. "They got nukes?"

His eyes widened.

"Well come on, I'm not stupid."

Sighing heavily, he took her upper arm in a gentle hand and steered her toward a giant boulder sitting nearby. She sat on it. He stood.

"None of that matters, because Tantilla is not in trouble and won't be if you agree to do this small job. You see, the president of Tantilla's daughter and her husband came to the U.S. on a diplomatic mission. They've been in D.C. for a week, and they were supposed to spend a week in Austin, but they disappeared."

Her eyes got bigger.

"Now I'm told they do this all the time. Run off to be alone together. It seems they're newlyweds who can't keep their hands off each other. They'll be found within a few days at most. In the meantime, it's in everyone's best interest that the U.S. keep it completely secret that they are missing.''

She blinked at him. ''How the hell do they plan to do that?''

''Put a couple in their place to attend social functions and photo ops, and basically fool the whole world for a matter of a few days. Just until we can track them down and get them back where they belong.''

She was frowning now as she thought this through. ''So someone's going to impersonate them?'' she asked.

He stared her in the eyes. ''Not someone. Us.''

She blinked. ''Us? As in you and me? But...but...''

He pulled something out of his coat. A photograph. She stared at it, but it was too dark. Then he was shining a penlight on it. The shot was of the most gorgeous couple she'd ever seen. The man was kind of hidden behind a beard and dark glasses, but the woman had the face of a movie star. Flawless features, stunning eyes, thick dark lashes and satiny raven hair, all softly curling around her face.

''Now do you see why I came to you?''

She looked up into his eyes, shaking her head slowly from side to side. ''No.''

He frowned at her. ''Mel, she could be your twin.''

Mel almost fell off the boulder. ''Huh?'' She looked down at the woman again, then back at him. ''You're kidding, right? She looks nothing like me.''

''She looks *exactly* like you. Your eyes, the shape of your nose, those cheekbones and that little pointy chin of yours. The dimples when you smile and the...''

Her gaze rose slowly to his. He looked away fast, cleared his throat. ''She's wearing makeup and has her hair done here. Trust me, with a makeup artist and hair-stylist, Katerina's own mother wouldn't be able to tell you apart."

"Katerina. That's her name."

He nodded. "The citizens call her Princess Katerina. She's very beloved."

Mel sighed, thinking it through. "I imagine she's also very educated, cultured and sophisticated, too."

"And soft-spoken, polite and gentle."

She was shaking her head slowly.

"We'll have a coach with you at all times. And I'll be with you."

"Playing…my husband."

"Yes. Thomas Antony Barde."

"I'll never pull off gentle and soft-spoken and polite in a million years, Alex."

"Katerina is shy. No one will question it if most of your responses are quiet smiles, or one- or two-word answers. I know you can do this, Mel."

"I don't know."

He licked his lips. Said nothing for a full minute. Then he said, "Yes. Tantilla has nukes. And its enemies don't like us. And if they find out Katerina and Thomas have taken off without their security team, they'll try to find them before we do. And they'll hurt them, or use them to force the president to hand over the country."

She closed her eyes. "Then I guess…I at least have to try. You promise you'll be with me all the way through?"

She thought he looked almost flooded with relief when he said, "Absolutely."

"Absolutely not!" Vidalia Brand said. She stomped her foot on the floor for emphasis, in case anyone thought she wasn't dead serious. "No daughter of mine is gonna go getting tangled up in some government espionage intrigue. No. It's too dangerous."

Alex did not like the fact that this gathering in the family room of Vidalia's home had taken on the characteristics of a full-blown Brand family meeting, but Caleb had been insistent that this was the way it had to be. So Maya and Caleb where there, their eighteen-month-old twins sleeping in the living room in a playpen. Edie and Wade were there, listening in and keeping mostly quiet, sitting very close. Kara and Selene were there, sitting side by side, looking worried. Mel was there, sitting by herself in a corner. They formed a loose circle, and he stood in the center to explain what he needed Mel to do. Vidalia Brand, the matriarch herself, was pacing back and forth now, shaking her head.

"It's not dangerous," Alex said again. "I'll be with her the whole time, and since everyone will believe Mel and I are the visiting dignitaries, we'll have Secret Service protection to boot."

"Besides all that, Mom," Mel said, "no one even knows the two are missing. And it's not like they've been kidnapped by terrorists or something. They're off on a lark. We're just gonna cover for them for a couple of days. It'll be…it'll be fun."

"Fun?" Vidalia asked.

Caleb got to his feet. "I wouldn't have let Alex approach Mel about this if I didn't believe it was safe, Vi. I promise you that. They're going to spend two or three days in a mansion being treated like royalty, dressing to the nines, going to parties. That's all this involves."

Vidalia looked at Caleb. Her face softened a little.

Caleb's father tapped his walking stick on the floor

three times. "Vidalia, key people involved in this will know what's going on."

"Like who?"

Sighing, Cain began to drop names, one of them belonging to a former president. Men Vidalia couldn't help but trust. Alex saw her giving in.

"Where would she be going? Washington, D.C.?"

"No," Alex said. "This is all happening in Austin."

"Where in Austin?"

"There's a house sometimes used for visiting dignitaries. We'll be staying there," Alex said.

"Have the place to yourselves, will you?"

He felt her eyes burning holes in him. "Well, not really. There will be a full staff, cooks and maids, drivers and bodyguards, and, of course, hair and makeup people for Mel."

"And a manners coach," Mel added.

Vidalia's brows rose. "Does that imply I haven't taught my daughter manners?" she asked Alex.

"Not at all, Mrs. Brand. Just not the same manners and mannerisms of a president's daughter."

Vidalia sniffed, thought, paced. Finally she went still. "I am nothing if not patriotic. The only things I love more than God and country are my daughters. So I'll let her do this thing on one condition."

"Name it," Alex said.

"I'm going with her. And Selene and Kara, too."

"I don't think—"

"You said there would be a staff. Well, we can be part of it. I'll do the cooking, and Selene and Kara can assist. Maya and Edie, with help from their respective husbands, and Cain here, can hold down the home front, run the saloon. Right?"

They all looked at her and nodded, though they might

as well have sent her a snappy salute. Alex got the feeling no one disagreed with this woman very often.

"That's the only way she's going. If I can go, too. Keep an eye on things."

Alex closed his eyes. This project was turning into a circus.

"We will not blow your cover, Alex," Selene said softly. She was the youngest, and her silver-blond hair and huge blue eyes were spooky. "We'll blend into the woodwork. No one will even notice us."

"Let them come, Alex," Mel said, getting to her feet. "They'll be good, I promise."

With a sigh, he gave in. But he had a feeling in the pit of his stomach telling him he would live to regret it.

Chapter 2

She had one day, the unflappable Alexander Stone told her, to get ready. A day. To figure out how the hell to look, speak, dress and act the part of a virtual princess. Apparently the famous Katerina's personal assistant was able to plead the couple out of a day's worth of commitments, with some fictional excuse.

She had a day to make herself into a totally different person. It was a lot to ask.

Vidalia put Alex up in the guest room, and he promised his "team" would arrive bright and early in the morning to get started. Get started on what? Mel wondered, visualizing Dorothy's visit to the salon in the land of Oz.

Someone was pounding on her bedroom door by the crack of dawn. She realized she must have slept soundly, all things considered, because she had a hell of a time waking up. Grumbling, she rolled over, pulling the covers over her head.

"I'm coming in, Melusine," a deep voice called from beyond the door.

The covers flipped off her face. "Huh?"

The door opened, and Alex peered in at her, then came the rest of the way. "Good, you're awake."

"Yeah, now."

"We want to get an early start. We have lots of ground to cover. You dressed under there?"

She lifted her eyebrows and nodded, wondering just where she ought to kick him first.

"Great. Why don't you hop in the shower, and we'll get set up? Okay?"

"We? You keep saying we. Who exactly do you—"

Again her bedroom door opened, and the woman who entered looked like a cartoon villainess.

"This is your personal maid, Katerina," Alex said softly, calling her by the stranger's name. "Bernadette is in charge of your wardrobe, your hair, your makeup and such."

"Oh." She looked at the imperious woman, disliking her instantly. "Hi. I'm Mel."

"No. You're Katerina," Bernadette said, her voice as stern as her silver-streaked black hair.

Mel bristled, getting to her feet. "I know who I am, lady."

"Bernadette works for the real Katerina. She's the only one outside our own people who knows what's going on. She's going to be coaching you on your mannerisms and behavior, as well."

"Oh, goodie," Mel said in a monotone.

"No one knows Katerina Belisle Barde the way I do, young lady. I know my job. Beginning now, and from this moment on, you answer only to Katerina or Madame Barde. Do you understand?"

Mel lifted her brows and tilted her head to one side. "And what do you answer to? Attila?"

The older woman narrowed her eyes on Mel in a way that had Mel feeling like a dalmatian pup. She glared right back at her, though.

"She's here to help you, Mel, er, Katerina," Alex muttered.

Pursing her lips, Mel gave a nod. "Fine. She can help me. But I won't be scolded or lectured or harassed. If I am, she's out the door." She faced the woman again. "Got it?"

"If you can't take direction, then there is no point in going forward at all," Bernadette informed her. "The proper response is, 'Yes, Bernadette. Of course I'll co-operate.'"

Mel stifled a laugh. "Yeah, in your dreams, lady."

The woman rolled her eyes heavenward.

Mel said, "Yes, Bernadette. Of course I'll cooperate with you. You just keep in mind here who's playing the princess and who's playing the servant, okay?" The woman's eyes widened and her face heated, but Mel ignored that, heading into the bathroom for her shower. And she locked the door behind her.

She took her shower quickly, in spite of having half a mind to linger, just to piss off the woman in the next room. Still, she felt a little guilty. Alex was probably realizing about now that Mel Brand and some delicate princess had less in common than a cactus and a tea rose.

When she was finished, she pulled on a terry robe, ran a brush through her still-wet hair and stepped back into her bedroom again.

The woman was gone. Alex was sitting on the edge of her bed waiting for her. There was a rack on wheels, suits and dresses hanging from it, shoes stacked beneath. On her dressing table were two small cases that stood opened, looking like miniature cosmetics counters, with tiered shelves and numerous drawers all lined with bottles, jars, tubes and devices.

"That was quick. I appreciate that," Alex said.

"I don't believe in long showers. Where is the wicked stepmother?"

He licked his lips, looked her up and down. "Sit down for a moment, would you? I want to show you something."

She bit back the sarcastic comment that popped instantly into mind and took a seat beside him on the bed. He had the remote to her portable TV/VCR combo in his hand, and he aimed it now and flicked a button.

A tape began playing. Footage of a graceful, beautiful woman who bore, in Mel's estimation, no more than a vague resemblance to her. She moved like a ballerina, had flawless skin, perfect manners, a shy, delicate way about her. She was soft-spoken and apparently shy. Kind and gentle.

Mel watched the woman step out of a palatial-looking building in a tropical clime and walk down a long walkway to where a gaggle of reporters waited. She spoke to them briefly, softly, shyly and then moved on to the waiting limousine. She made getting into the back of a car look like choreography.

The screen went black.

Mel sighed. "I'm never, ever going to pull it off."

"Not by yourself, no. But if you let this woman—this *expert*—help you, you'll do it in spades, Mel. I know you will."

She licked her lips. "I'll try."

"There's a lot at risk. Don't try. Just do it."

She nodded slowly. "All right."

"All right." He got to his feet and opened the bedroom door. "My wife is ready for you now."

"Right away, Mr. Barde."

She blinked away the feeling of oddness, the surreal sense that she was playing a child's game in a very grown-up way, and this time she received her personal assistant with a smile designed to be gentle like the one she had seen the real Katerina beam at everyone she encountered.

Alex left Mel in Bernadette's capable hands and headed downstairs. In the kitchen, hovering over their morning coffee, Vidalia, Kara and Selene awaited him. Vidalia got up, poured him a cup and then nodded at him to sit.

"So how did that one go over with Mel?" she asked.

"There were some…tense moments, but they seem to be getting along now."

"Humph. I knew she and Mel were gonna clash. She's too bossy."

"Mom, we have to call her Katerina, remember?" It was Selene, the youngest, gently reminding her mother. "We agreed to do this exactly the way we're asked."

"Yeah, and so did Mel," Kara put in. Then she bit her lip. "I mean, Katerina. Gosh, this is gonna be hard."

"But you're right, Kara. She did agree, and now she's gonna have to swallow her temper and her pride and just do what needs doing," Selene said.

Vidalia nodded. "It's just as well we'll be there to help her." She looked to Alex. "She gets huffy on you, you just let me know. I'll take care of it in short order."

Alex had to stifle a smile. He could see a lot of Mel's

mother in her. A strong woman, and very honest. He thought about the women in his social circle, women who were so good at artifice that you never knew what they were really thinking. Any one of them could have easily played the role of princess, but he doubted any of them would be willing to go to the trouble to do so.

Not so with this bunch.

"So," Vidalia asked as he took a sip of the delicious coffee, "exactly what are the sleeping arrangements going to be with you two?"

He choked, and yanked a paper napkin to his mouth just in time to prevent the coffee from spattering the kitchen table. Thank goodness for that tacky rooster-shaped wooden napkin holder in the center.

"I am her mother. I have a right to ask."

"From this moment on, you are her cook. And mine. Please, Vidalia, you have to try to get into the right mindset."

"That is one very clever way to change the subject, Mr. Stone."

"Mr. Barde," he corrected. "Thomas Barde."

She crossed her arms over her chest and stared at him. He gave up and told her, "I haven't seen the house yet, but rest assured, I am a professional and I take my work very seriously. I'm not going to compromise your daughter." Not in this lifetime. "I'm going to do the job I was hired to do. That may entail creating the illusion of intimacy between us, especially since the couple we're impersonating are madly in love and only recently married. But rest assured that even if you see things that cause you concern, they will not be real. It's a cover, Mrs. Brand. And it's one that's necessary for our national security. All right?"

"I have your word on that?"

"You do."

She nodded slowly.

"How do you suppose they're doing upstairs?" Selene asked.

"Oh, they'll be a while. Unless our dear Katerina kills Bernadette and puts an early stop to things." Even as he said it, there was a growling shout from above, followed by a string of obscenities in Mel's unmistakable voice.

"My heavens, what is that woman doing to her?"

"It's just a guess," Selene said. "But I'd say they're waxing."

Sighing, shaking her head, Vidalia got up, walked into the living room and stopped at the foot of the stairs. "Melusine Brand! I mean, Katerina Barde, you watch your ever-lovin' mouth, young lady!"

From above, another bellow came, but this time the words that followed were muted and unintelligible.

Mel couldn't believe her eyes when the women finished the torture session two hours later. She stood in front of the full-length mirror in her room, wearing not her usual faded jeans but a shell-pink skirt and tailored jacket, with a sleeveless white silk blouse underneath. Her stockings were silk, too, and the pearly pink pumps matched the pearls around her neck and on her earlobes. Her eyebrows had been plucked and shaped into perfect arches, and the makeup made the deep blue of her eyes look even deeper and her already thick lashes look even thicker and her cheekbones—well, hell, she'd never even noticed her cheekbones before.

Bernadette was still fussing with her hair. She'd added some auburn and burgundy highlights to the deep black waves, giving it shimmering shades that changed in the light.

The woman stood back admiring her work, nodding silently in approval. Mel stared at herself in the mirror. "This isn't me," she whispered.

"It is for a few days, Katerina," Bernadette said softly. "But the makeup and clothes are the easy parts. You'll have help. Hair and makeup girls newly hired to assist you during your stay. I'll supervise, of course, but they will believe you to be the real Katerina. Your appearance will never be a problem so long as you trust us to help you. The rest is going to be much more difficult."

"More difficult than having tiny hairs torn from various parts of my body?"

The woman actually smiled. "You have the spirit to do this. And the beauty was already there. I only enhanced it. You fit Katerina's clothing to a T. The rest is just a matter of thinking, always thinking. Before you speak, before you move, before you act, always think. Ask yourself, is this something Katerina Barde would say or do? Is this the way she would move? Take your time and then proceed. If you observe ladies of breeding and social status, you'll notice they always move slowly and deliberately and gracefully. Hurrying is your enemy."

"You make it sound easy."

"Walk for me. Cross the room, then turn and come back."

Taking a deep breath, Mel turned and walked the length of the room, making her steps as slow and as graceful as she knew how. Then she turned and came back.

The woman nodded. "Good. Good. Already you're

thinking ahead. Let's polish it now. Each foot is placed precisely in front of the other. So your footprints would form a straight line if you could see them. And you need to keep your head up, chin up, don't look down at your feet as you walk. And don't swing your arms so much. They should be almost still. All right?''

''Straight line, arms still, chin up.''

''And smile.''

She grimaced instead, then straightened her posture and tried the walk again, feeling like a kid playing at being a princess.

Bernadette applauded this time. She did not do so by clapping both hands together, but by cupping one hand and slapping the four fingers of the other one against it repeatedly. Mel made a mental note.

''Now, let's work on sitting.''

''Sitting?'' Mel asked.

So they worked on sitting. And on getting up. And then they practiced talking, asking and answering questions without really saying much at all. The tone, always soft, the eyes always direct, the grammar always correct.

For hours they worked, and Mel knew it was just the beginning. Hell, she was going to hate this. She knew she was.

There was a knock on the door. Bernadette leaned close to Mel and whispered, ''Enter.''

''Enter,'' Mel called in her newfound Katerina voice, all soft as a breeze.

The door opened, and a man stood there. He had a very short, very neat beard on his chin, and he wore dark sunglasses and a shiny suit that looked as if it had probably cost more than her own entire wardrobe. Not

Katerina's but Mel's. Good grief, she was going to develop a split personality.

He stared at her for a moment, not saying anything. Then finally he seemed to snap out of it. "Ah, Katerina," he said, smiling at her. "You are a picture of beauty, just as always." He strode toward her, took her hand in his and brought it to his mouth, which was a very sexy mouth, especially when it was spewing flattery at her in an accent that was kind of British but with a touch of something hotter and more Latin flavoring it.

"I...I..."

He released her hand, and his own rose to remove the amber-tinted sunglasses. She met his eyes and then blinked her own. *"Alex?"*

Bernadette glared at her.

"Uh, that is, I mean, Thomas. My...husband. You look...and you...so..." She stopped there, her eyes widening, and she turned to face Bernadette. "Wait a minute, what about the accent? Am I supposed to have one, too? How am I going to fool anyone without an accent?"

"Katerina attended private schools in the U.S. from the ninth grade on, including university. She has barely any discernable accent at all."

"But I do," Mel insisted. "I sound like an Oklahoman!"

"Actually, you don't," Bernadette said. "At least, not when you're in character. I expected it would be a problem, but you seem to lose it naturally when you're speaking as Katerina Barde."

"I do?"

"Yes. I assumed you had done some training for the stage."

She shook her head, bewildered.

"You might just be channeling her, Mel," Selene said from out in the hallway, peering into the bedroom. "You really look like her, you know."

"You look…incredible," Alex said.

Mel met his eyes. "I do not look incredible. *This* is not me. I do not look like this. Katerina looks incredible, and I simply look like Katerina. Given the choice, Alex, I'd be in my jeans, with my face scrubbed clean and my feet bare and the wind blowing my hair any way it pleased."

He blinked when she said that and looked away from her. "I wasn't trying to insult you. It was a compliment."

"It was Katerina's compliment, not mine. Give it to her when you see her."

He faced her again, his brows crinkled as if he were puzzled.

"Never mind," she said.

"Calm," Bernadette said, snapping the word out like a command, even while patting Mel's shoulder. "Get back into your role."

The woman was a damn drill sergeant. Mel drew a breath, straightened, lifted her chin and pasted Katerina's wishy-washy smile on her face. "Shall we go to dinner, darling? We do have a long flight ahead."

He looked at her for a moment, perhaps taken aback by the sudden change. But he quickly followed suit, falling back into his own role seemingly without effort. "Of course, love." He offered his arm.

She took it, then did the princess walk out of her room and down the stairs. Despite hating every second of this make-believe crap, Mel thought she had never heard anything sexier than Alexander Stone speaking in that phony accent. And the beard did things to his face. Made him look a little less polished and polite, a little more dangerous and unpredictable.

But she had to remember that he, too, was simply playing a role.

Selene watched the two of them go down the stairs, shaking her head slowly. ''This can't lead to anything good,'' she muttered to no one in particular.

Chapter 3

"Now remember, the cover story is that we flew out so that you could visit a friend back in Tantilla who was in the hospital. Her name is not being released to protect her privacy. Naturally, never wishing to be far from your side, I went with you. Now we're back and ready to resume our schedule here in Austin."

Alex sat beside her in the small plane and kept his voice low, so that the "staff," who rode farther back, wouldn't overhear. That staff included some newly hired hair and makeup people, her mother and two of her sisters, and Bernadette. Their security team would be waiting at the airport.

"How is she doing now?" Mel asked.

Alex lifted his head, looked at her blankly. "Who?"

"My friend who was in the hospital. How is she doing? I mean, I need to know how to act when I'm asked about her. Did she have a heart attack or a baby? Is she alive? Comatose? Treated and released?"

He closed his eyes. "Which would you prefer?"

She thought a moment. "She had a baby. Twins. I'm experienced with that. I won't need to lie so much. And they're all doing just fine."

He nodded. "It's a good story."

"We'll be landing in two minutes," the pilot announced.

"Oh, God." Mel's hand tightened on the armrest between her and Alex. His hand slid over hers, rested there.

"Don't be nervous. This is gonna be fine, I promise."

Swallowing hard, she nodded.

A short while later, Mel stepped out of the small airplane with Alex right behind her. From the moment they started down the steps, he was close to her, one arm around her waist, hand resting on her hip, as if she were too delicate to walk down the stairs by herself. She knew he didn't like her very much, and she guessed it must be tough on him to try to play the role of adoring husband.

Her entourage came behind her, but she resisted the urge to turn and look back at her mother or sisters in search of reassurance. She and Bernadette and Alex had been over and over this routine. Together they had watched countless tapes of Katerina and Thomas. They clung to each other, fawned over each other. Nothing vulgar, no public necking, but it seemed wherever they went they were always touching, always making eye contact, exchanging secret little messages and long, lingering looks. The two were utterly dopey about each other. It was easy behavior to emulate. Especially when Alex was wearing the beard and talking in that accent. She could do this. She could pretend he was someone she was utterly crazy about.

She plastered a smile on her face, drawing a little more warmth from Alex's physical proximity than was probably wise. They reached the tarmac, and the arm around her waist retreated, replaced by the more proper bent arm at his side, which she took hold of with both hands—an impulse move. He glanced down at her, smiled a little. She smiled back, tried to feign an adoring gaze.

"Nice touch," he whispered.

Together they walked ahead, to the place where men and women, the political elite of Texas, formed a gauntlet she was supposed to run. To the far left and right of her, she saw the Secret Service agents, and she felt Alex tense.

"What is it?" she whispered from behind her smile.

"Nothing."

"You know one of them, don't you?"

He glanced down, gave a slight nod. "Just stay in the role. We're fine."

They approached the waiting dignitaries. Each took her hand in greeting, then took Alex's. Each offered some version of "Welcome back to Texas." She nodded, smiled, returned their grips with a firm one, but not too firm, and said, "Thank you, we're so happy to be here," more times than she cared to count.

"My goodness," one woman said. "You look so fresh after such a long flight. How do you do it?"

"Long flight? But it was only—" Alex's hand patted hers where it rested on his arm.

"We have so little time alone together," he said, in that sexy accent. He gazed down at her, his eyes warm behind the tinted glasses. "I'm afraid the flight seemed all too brief."

Her tummy fluttered a little. She silently reminded

herself that this was pretend. Then she lowered her head and lashes, as if embarrassed.

The woman laughed and beamed at them.

A limo pulled to a stop ahead. The rear doors opened, and the agents hustled them toward it. Alex stood back while Mel faced away from the car, lowered her delicate rump onto the seat, smoothing her skirt with one hand, then drew her legs in as one, toes pointed. She had practiced getting in and out of the car 150 times in the driveway of her own home before they'd headed to the airport.

She saw, too, Bernadette's approving look as she and the rest of the "staff" got into other waiting vehicles.

Alex slid in beside her. The door closed, and the limo pulled away.

Mel leaned back in the seat, closed her eyes and sighed in relief.

The divider window slid open, and the driver said, "Very nice job."

Alex went tense, his hand sliding to his side, giving Mel the impression that he carried a gun there. Of course he did. She should have realized. Mel covered his hand with hers, though, as she caught the driver's face reflected in the rearview mirror. He was darkly handsome, Native American—and familiar.

"Wait a minute, I—do I know you?"

"Wes Brand. Welcome to Texas, cuz."

"Brand?" Alex asked, shooting a puzzled look from Mel to the driver and back again.

Ignoring Alex, Mel blinked in surprise. "Wes? Oh my God, I haven't seen anyone from your side of the family since—gosh, since I was five or six years old."

"Too long," Wes said. "Way too long. I figured it was high time we fixed that."

"Would someone mind explaining to me just what the hell is going on?"

She glanced at Alex, who looked ready to kill someone. "Wes is my cousin. One of a whole pile of cousins, the Texas Brands."

"There's more of us all the time," Wes said. Then he met Alex's gaze in the rearview. "Vidalia called us. And don't go getting angry about it. She's concerned about Mel's safety."

"It's a matter of national security," Alex said. "My God, how many of you people know about this?"

"Just Garrett and I. Garrett's the sheriff of Quinn, and you can trust us both with this information. We realized Vidalia was breaking protocol by confiding in us, and we knew better than to spread it around. But we also felt it couldn't hurt to have one of us inside, keeping an eye on the situation just in case." He sent Mel a wink. "Estranged or not, Mel's family."

"I can't even believe you did this for me." Mel couldn't stop smiling. "We've got so much to catch up on! You know, this job might not be as miserable as I thought it would be."

Alex rolled his eyes and sat back in his seat while Mel and Wes Brand talked about family, cousins, marriages, babies. Mel knew he was angry, but she didn't really care. She felt safer, more confident, having Wes there. Even though she barely knew him, she knew he was family. A Brand. And in the Brand family, family came first.

It was the code they all lived by. And though Mel's own branch of the family had been estranged from the Texas branch for a long time now, they'd never questioned one another's commitment to that unspoken vow.

It came with the Brand name.

She trusted her kin. More than she trusted anyone else. Including the man sitting beside her right now.

"I can have you off this job and back on your ranch with a phone call," Alex said to Wes. "I could probably have you behind bars just as easily."

Wes's eyes narrowed in the mirror. "You can try."

"No, no, look, there's no need for this," Mel said quickly. "Alex, he said they didn't tell anyone else. And—well, hell, I feel safer having Wes here. I mean, Mom and the girls are one thing. But in my family I'm the tough one. I'm the protector. With Wes, I feel like there's someone else around to look out for me."

Alex slanted her a sideways glance. "That's what I'm here to do."

Wes looked up sharply from the front seat. "Oh. Now I get it."

"Get what?" Alex asked, and his tone was not friendly.

"Hey, ease off, will you?" Wes snapped. "I'm her cousin."

"What the hell does that have to do with anything?"

The two faced off via the rearview until Wes had to jerk his eyes to the road again. "The way I see it," he said, speaking slowly, "one more set of eyes watching over Mel can't hurt things. And it *could* help. At least there's no question whose side I'm on."

"We're all on the same side."

"Not exactly," Wes said. "All the other shadowy characters you've got working this thing are on the government's side. I'm on Mel's."

"And you think I'm not?" Alex asked.

"I haven't decided yet."

Mel put a hand on Alex's shoulder. "Please let him stay."

"No."

Her face tensed. She felt it heat as her temper rose to dangerous levels. "Fine. Stop the car, Wes."

"Huh?"

"Stop the car. You and I are getting out. Right here, right now."

"Mel," Alex began

"Screw you, Alex. I've been taking all the crap you and your damn makeover maven have been dishing out for twenty-four hours, all because you say my country needs me. Well, my country may need me, but if all it can do is use me, then it can go to hell, and you can go with it."

Alex stared at her, gaping for a long moment. Wes was still driving, but he had slowed down considerably. Finally Alex leaned his head against the seat back. "Keep driving. You can stay."

Mel grated her teeth. No apology. Hell, no, that would be a freaking miracle. But at least he'd surrendered. She forced the words to her mouth, though they tasted like bile coming out. "Thank you."

He said nothing.

The car pulled into the circular drive. Agents were already there, so Alex knew the place was secure. One of them opened Mel's door. She slipped back into character immediately, stretching her long, shapely legs out, alighting from the car with ease. She was good at this, he admitted to himself grudgingly. And so damn stunning to look at that he doubted anyone would notice a slip anyway. She waited for him to emerge, and he did, standing close enough to her that their hips were touching, an arm lightly around her waist. He automatically scanned the area, his eyes sharp from long practice.

Some habits didn't break easily. Mel might think he was useless, and he fully admitted he probably would be at ranching or roping bulls or wilderness camping. He was not a cowboy. Had never claimed to be. But he was a damn fine Secret Service agent, one of the best before he resigned. He could protect her better than anyone he knew. If she couldn't see that, then fine. He really didn't care.

Seeing nothing to alarm him, he started forward, toward the walk and the steps to the front door, but Mel hesitated.

He glanced down at her and saw the wonder in her eyes as she stared at the house in which they were to be staying for the next few days. He'd thought it nothing so unusual. Just another Georgian manor like so many in the area. But he looked at it again now, trying to see it through her eyes. Her little farmhouse in Oklahoma could fit inside this one four times over. While her own lawn at home was kept neatly mowed and was dotted with plots of daffodils and petunias, this one was professionally manicured, completely fenced in and included a flagstone path, fountains and cement figures of Greek deities.

It must seem like a palace to her. However, it wouldn't to Katerina. He squeezed her just a bit closer. "I know it's not what you're used to, my love. But it will do, yes?"

She blinked away the look of awe and smiled at him. "Smaller only means we'll remain closer to each other."

A camera flashed. She didn't flinch, just averted her face and picked up her gait a bit. A second later they were inside, closing the doors behind themselves, locking them. She started to relax the second they were in the house, he saw it when she pulled free of his loosely linked arm and sighed, looking around the place.

He snagged her again, pulled her close to him and held her cradled to his chest, even as she tensed. "Shh. Stay in character," he whispered. With one hand he cupped the back of her head, bending as if to nuzzle her ear but really the better to whisper words she could hear. "There's always an outside chance the place could be bugged."

"And you need to make love to me in the living room in order to whisper to me?" she hissed back.

"Look at the windows."

She did, and saw what he wanted her to see. The faces several yards beyond, straining to see inside. Reporters with cameras and zoom lenses. Mel's arms closed around him, palms flat to his back. She pressed her face closer to his ear. "So we have to do this any time we want to speak freely?"

"You complaining?"

"As if I'd be the first?"

He smiled. He couldn't help it. She was good at sparring, and he enjoyed it. "Yes, you *would* be the first, as a matter of fact."

"You should count yourself lucky, Al. Any other man groped me the way you're doing, I'd incapacitate him. Maybe permanently."

"I know, I've seen you in action."

"So you gonna let go of me now?"

"I don't know."

"Why not?"

"You smell good."

She bit his earlobe, and, God help him, he liked it. But it startled him enough so that he let her go. But when he did, she was smiling, and he thought it was genuine this time, not part of her act. She'd been tense in the car. So had he, and he'd hoped to ease it by teasing her a little. Maybe he'd succeeded.

"Thomas, what about the staff?" she asked in her Katerina-soft tones, even as she walked to the front windows and gently drew the drapes closed.

"They've been fully briefed by now, my love. Just as we have. I'm sure they know where everything is and are already settling into their routine."

"May we check in on them?"

"Of course." He knew she was concerned about her mother and sisters settling into all of this. He led her through the massive house, through large, opulent rooms into the more mundane parts in the back. There were a kitchen, bathrooms, a living area and a dining room clearly intended for the house staff. A separate stairway led to their bedrooms upstairs. They found the gang sitting around a small kitchen table, notepads in front of them. Vidalia, Selene and Kara all wore the same turquoise dresses as Sophie and Sally, the new hair and makeup girls. Bernadette wore a chic-looking black suit. Wes was dressed in a navy suit.

"Thomas, Katerina! You needn't have come, I was going to come and brief you as soon as I had finished with the staff," Bernadette said, rising from her seat.

Alex held up a hand, indicating they should remain seated. "My wife wanted to assure herself you had all arrived and have everything you need."

"Like the gracious princess she is," Vidalia quipped, a mischievous light in her eyes. Kara elbowed her and suppressed a giggle.

Bernadette sent them a look but quickly returned her attention to the "newlyweds." "I have your schedule for you. If you'd like to go over it now…?"

"Yes, please, I would very much like to," Mel said.

"Very good, then." Bernadette flipped pages in her notepad. "Luncheon will be with the ladies of the Freedom Alliance. You'll be speaking at that function, Katerina. I have your speech prepared." She bent to a case beside her and pulled out a sheaf of papers, handing it to Mel. "After that you have three interviews with the press lined up this afternoon, at two, three and four o'clock respectively, and then a state dinner tonight at seven, hosted by the mayor."

Mel only looked at her. Then at Alex. Then at the speech in her hand.

"Three interviews is too much, Bernadette," Alex said. "After all, it's only our first day. Cancel them and tell the press to expect a written statement instead, all right?"

Bernadette nodded firmly, scribbling in her notepad. "Done."

He glanced at Mel. She was a little on the pale side. "I think you should rest before the luncheon, take the time to go over your speech, hmm?"

She nodded.

"We're going to find our room," he told them. Vidalia sent him a warning glance. He gave her what he hoped was a reassuring nod and turned Mel to guide her back through the house and up the wide stairs to the second floor.

It wasn't difficult to find the master suite. He'd been given the layout of the house in advance and had committed it to memory. He flung open the double doors at the far end of the main hall and led her into the wide sitting room. It included a fireplace, laid ready for lighting, a glass-topped coffee table, surrounded by French provincial chairs and a settee. In another section of the room, a nook surrounded on three sides by windows, there were a small dining table and a pair of chairs. He didn't stop there, though she would have. In fact, she started to head to the settee, but he clasped her hand and pulled her along behind him, through the next door that led to the opulent bedroom, with its four-poster bed piled high with mattresses, pillows, bolsters. The comforter was powder blue, to match the bedskirt. The bed was so high it had a footstool beside it for easier access.

She planted her feet, her eyes glued to that bed.

He held her eyes, shook his head once and tugged her into motion again. Through another door, the bathroom waited. As large as Mel's living room at home, it held a sunken tub, a separate shower big enough for more than one occupant at a time, and a bubbling redwood hot tub near the windows.

After closing the door behind him, Alex walked around turning on all the faucets and flipping the switches that started the overhead fans running. When he came back to her, she was sitting on the steps to the hot tub.

"The last place anyone would bug would be the private bath," he said. "It's small enough that we can sweep it easily and often, and it's too easy for us to drown out our voices with all the water and fans." He sat down beside her. "Still, keep your voice down."

Drawing a troubled breath, she lifted her gaze to his. "They expect me to give speeches and interviews?" Her eyes were wide, and their color, that dark sapphire blue with darker midnight stripes, held his attention. He hadn't noticed those stripes before. They drew him in. "You never told me that, Alex. I wasn't expecting it."

"There's nothing to it. Your speech is written for you. All you need to do is read it."

She blinked at him, so his eyes broke their hold. "That's easy for you to say. Public speaking is not something I've ever been able to deal with. I almost failed high school English because of it. Part of the final exam was an oral presentation. I thought I would die up there."

He just looked at her for a long moment, waiting for the punch line. But it didn't come. "You are the most aggressive, opinionated, in-your-face person I've ever known. You're telling me you suffer from stage fright?"

She nodded.

"Even having the speech in front of you to read won't help?"

"I tried that once. I lost my place and got so nervous I dropped the notes all over the floor. Everyone laughed."

"And you didn't beat them up for that?"

"As many as I could find during the following week, but it didn't help right then."

He hadn't expected her to answer the question and almost laughed at the reply. But he could see she was really dreading this.

"And what will I do if they ask questions after?" she asked. "About things I don't know?"

"All right, all right. Listen, I have an idea. Can you give me an hour? Just lie down, rest, relax, paint your toenails or something."

She shot him a glare. He ran a hand over her hair and then wondered why he'd done it. "I'll fix this. I promise."

She swallowed hard, nodding. "An hour," she said.

"But make some of those bulldogs out there keep everyone away. If I have some VIP visitor and you're not here with me, I'll probably throw up on their three-hundred-dollar shoes."

He smiled and closed his eyes. "Ahh, it's nice to be needed."

She chucked him in the shoulder.

Sighing, he got to his feet. "You ready to be the princess again?"

"Yeah, so long as you have a shot of insulin nearby."

He cranked off the faucets, turned off the fans. The room went silent. Mel sighed and started to get up. Alex gripped her hands and gave a tug. She seemed tired. Not physically, though he imagined that running around in designer wear and heels was no picnic for her, either. But this was an emotional tiredness, and it was way too soon for her to be feeling it.

He opened the door, led her back into the bedroom, to the bed. She sat down on its edge, kicked off the shoes and flopped backward like a ragdoll.

"I'll see you in an hour," he said, in character.

"I can hardly wait." She clapped a hand over her mouth, but Alex only smiled and shook his head. He doubted anyone but him picked up the sarcasm in her tone. Then he left.

She dreamed a version of Rogers and Hammerstein's *Cinderella,* with her as the lead. Wearing a gown, a tiara and a pair of delicate glass slippers, she kicked her stepsisters' asses, tossed her stepmother into the moat, and told the prince to quit acting like such a gentleman and just kiss her already.

He obliged, of course. His mouth on hers was so

warm and so real. His arms around her, familiar and
protective. When he lifted his head, she was in rags,
covered in soot, barefoot. He looked at her and said,
"Oh, this will never do."

"But all the rest was make-believe," she argued.
"This is who I really am. Not a princess. Just an ordinary girl."

"Ordinary girls can't marry princes," he told her.

Anger suffused her entire body. She was so hot with
it that she woke up, sat up in the bed and found herself
glaring at the man who was standing just inside the
door.

"What?" Alex asked, searching her face.

She blinked, realizing that the prince in the dream
had been Alex. Or Thomas. Or some sick blend of the
two. Sighing, she shook her head. "Nothing. Have you
been able to solve the problem we discussed?"

"Of course I did. I promised you I would, didn't I?"
He was using his accent. It rubbed her nerve endings in
a good way. A dangerous way.

He came to the bed, sat on its edge beside her and
opened his hand. In his palm was a pair of earrings.
Twin ice-blue sapphires the size of Florida cockroaches.
"For you, my precious flower." He leaned closer, close
enough so that his breath fanned her neck, and clipped
an earring on her ear. His lips touched her sensitive skin
there as he whispered, "It's a wireless communication
device. I'll be able to speak to you, and you'll hear me.
I can talk you through the speech, feed you lines, whatever you need me to do."

She shivered, because his mouth so close to her ear
was doing things to her. Nice things. Things she knew
better than to indulge. When he pulled away, she
wanted more, so she leaned up to his ear and gave like

for like. She let her lips brush him as she whispered, "Can you hear me, as well as speak to me?"

He gripped her shoulders, set her back just slightly from him and reached into his pocket. He pulled out a matching pendant on a golden chain, hooked it around her neck and nodded at her.

So the pendant was a microphone and the earring an earpiece. And she was turned on by Mr. *GQ*. Gosh, so many revelations all at once.

"Thank you, my love. You're so good to me."

"Nothing is too good for you, darling," he replied. "It's nearly time for that luncheon. Shall I send your maids up?"

"Yes, I...I suppose."

He frowned, probably at her seeming reluctance. "We'll have plenty of time to be alone together tonight, Katerina. I know it's difficult to wait, but we have promises to keep."

She narrowed her eyes on him and mouthed, "In your dreams."

He shrugged, and his eyes were grinning with mischief, even though his mouth remained firm. Then he turned and left her there.

She knew what he was doing. Whenever she felt panic coming on, he would say something to either piss her off or make her laugh, or both. He was good at it, which wasn't surprising.

What *was* surprising was that he always seemed to know when she felt panic coming on. He read her face, or...or something.

It was odd. She didn't think she liked it.

Chapter 4

The banquet hall was huge, with every seat and table filled. At the front stood a podium with a microphone, and behind that, a wall. Behind the wall was another section, kind of a backstage area, where Mel paced nervously. She was supposed to have arrived in time to enjoy luncheon with the ladies of the Freedom Alliance. Instead, here she was with Alex, peering out at them and getting more nervous by the minute. She'd pleaded a queasy stomach to one of the organizers and asked if she could just wait backstage until it was time to go on. It hadn't even been a lie.

"Have you even looked at the speech?" Alex asked.

"No. Every time I try, I feel like throwing up." She shrugged. "I thought it would be best to just read it cold."

Alex stepped closer, pressed the heel of his hand to her back, right in between her shoulder blades. She pushed back against it, and he rubbed small circles there, easing her somewhat.

"Feels good," she muttered, closing her eyes. "So just what is this group about, anyway? Freedom Alliance? What do they do?"

"Politicians' wives with time on their hands, for the most part. But they do some good work. Their last major fund-raiser generated about a hundred grand for Afghan women."

Mel opened her eyes, lifted her brows. "Yeah, but how much of it got to the women?"

"I think they do pretty well in that regard. Very low overhead. All volunteers."

She nodded. "So I'm guessing they didn't just send a check."

"Supplies. Food, fabric, sewing machines, clothes, staples like that."

"I hope they included a nice big baseball bat for each woman, just in case the men over there get out of line again."

His hand stilled, which made her look up over her shoulder at him. She caught him smiling at her from behind his beard. It warmed her insides in a way it shouldn't have done. She shrugged and looked away, then went stiff when she realized the meal was over and the emcee was taking her place at the podium.

"I'm going to be in that small room, right back there," Alex said, pointing until she followed his finger to the little door a few yards away. "You'll be fine. I'll never be out of touch. If you get stuck, just pause, take a sip of water to stall for time, and I'll whisper in your ear. I have a copy of the speech, so I can cue you if you lose your place. Nothing can go wrong."

She nodded stiffly, scared to death. "Do I look all right?"

He looked her up and down. "Beyond all right. You look beautiful. Like a princess should look."

"But not like a Brand girl from Oklahoma should look," she whispered. She fingered the tailored dress. It was powder blue, with shoes to match. Her hair had been sprayed to within an inch of its life, her nails and makeup done to perfection. "I feel like a department-store mannequin."

"But you might be saving your country."

She rolled her eyes. "Has anyone had any luck finding the other two?"

"Not yet. It's only been a day. Be patient."

"Patient. They're probably having sex in a hot tub in Aspen or something, while I sweat it out here playing princess games. If I ever see them, don't think I'm not going to give them hell for this."

"I don't doubt it."

He was still smiling. She was amusing him, she thought. "Bernie says there's a ball tomorrow night in our honor. A *ball*."

"Bernie?"

"Bernadette," she finally clarified.

He searched her face for a long moment, then it split in a smile.

She smiled back. She couldn't help it. When the man smiled, he was freaking devastating.

"That's better," he told her. "Try to keep smiling out there. Just pause every once in a while, look out at the crowd and flash that killer smile. You'll have them in the palm of your hand."

Beyond the wall, a woman's voice was rattling off a long and honor-filled introduction. Someone came through the small open door through which Mel had been peeking now and then, and motioned for her to come forward.

Alex clasped her shoulder. "You'll be wonderful out there. And I'll be with you." He patted his pocket, where she knew he had a small headset tucked away. Then he headed toward the room in the back.

Mel heard Katerina Belisle Barde's name spoken into the microphone, heard a groundswell of applause, stiffened her spine and put a picture of bald eagles swooping over American flags in her mind, with fireworks going off in the background. She tried to think of some patriotic tune as she marched out onto the stage, but her mind would only repeat instructions on how to walk properly, stand properly, hold her head properly, interspersed with quips about smiling and making eye contact.

She wished she had at least glanced at the speech. And what if the equipment failed? What if she couldn't hear Alex? She started breathing a little faster as she walked to the podium, forcing a fake smile. Cupping one hand over the microphone, she whispered from behind clenched teeth, "Are you there? Say something, dammit."

He didn't *say* anything. He gave a soft wolf whistle. Soft laughter bubbled up from her chest, and she lowered her head to hide it.

"That's better," the voice in her ear said. "Now hold up a hand to stop the applause and say thank you for that warm welcome and how glad you are to be here."

She held up her hand, and the applause slowly died. "Thank you so much. I cannot tell you how happy I am to be here. You've all been so very kind to my husband and me. It's truly an honor to be here."

"Now just start reading," Alex instructed.

She glanced down at her notes, using a forefinger to mark the line. "With help from its allies, my country has come a long, long way since the dictator Curnyn Shaw was ousted from power. My father and his cabinet are well aware that we still have a long way to go. But things are very promising. Our economy is finally showing signs of stability and even growth. Our schools are clean and safe, and our health-care systems have been vastly improved over the past year. I can report to you now, today, that all of Tantilla's school-age children have been properly immunized and seen by a doctor or nurse practitioner for a routine physical examination. Those found to have health problems are being treated. As you know, the children are one of my main areas of concern in my nation, and I am so pleased to be able to report this progress to you."

When she glanced down at the page, her finger was still way up, even though she knew she had read all the way down. She tapped her pendant, took a sip of water, and beamed a smile at the crowd.

"Third line from the bottom," Alex whispered into her ear. "As for the women..."

She found the spot easily. "As for the women in my country," Mel read, finding herself interested to read on, "change, I fear, comes a bit more slowly in this area. People are very set in their ways in regard to gender roles." Frowning, she flipped the page, even as she heard Alex mutter something that sounded like, "Oh, hell."

She pretended to sip water. "What was that?" she muttered.

"Nothing, just keep reading. You are Katerina. Don't forget that. Now read."

She lowered the glass, smiled, looked at the page. "Women cannot simply be granted, all at once, rights they've never before had. We must prepare them first to properly understand how to handle those rights, and, likewise, we must prepare the men for the repercussions of this change. Within five years we hope to grant all women the right to have a driver's license and to own property. The vote will take a bit longer, as you know, because this...this is complete bull."

A gasp went up from the crowd.

She looked up sharply.

"What the hell are you doing?" Alex demanded in her ear. "Mel, don't—"

She yanked off the earring. "I am the daughter of the president of Tantilla. Apparently, in my country, that means that I can speak only my father's thoughts, because women don't seem to be perceived as capable of having thoughts and minds of their own. Yet, here I am, in a room surrounded by strong, powerful, independent American women. Can you imagine how your government would react to my nation if it were denying these same basic human rights to people based on their race or ethnicity? Or to the very old? Or to one religious group? But it's only the women being denied their rights. Does that make it acceptable? No! I think not!"

"Mel, for the love of God!" Alex said from the doorway in the wall, but she could barely hear him for the rousing applause filling the room.

When it quieted, she spoke again. "Personally, I feel the United States government should refuse all aid to Tantilla until and unless it presents the U.S. with a workable, fair and fast plan to see to it that women stop being treated as property. No exceptions. No delays. No giving the men time to get used to the idea. Have you ever heard anything more farfetched than that pile of—''

Alex was beside her now, his hand closing on her shoulder in a firm grip. "Get back in character," he whispered in her ear. "And for God's sake, wrap it up."

She nodded. "If the women of Tantilla had wanted to live under the yoke of discrimination, then my country might as well have left Curnyn in power. But we didn't. Tantilla is free!" she said, pounding her fist on the podium. "Tantilla is a democracy!" She pounded it again. "Now the world must demand that it behave like one!"

The roomful of women burst into wild applause so loud the room vibrated with it. They rose to their feet as one, and suddenly cameras were flashing. Mel came out of the moment briefly to look at herself. That earring was clasped in her fist as she shook it in the air.

Alex had his arm around her shoulders in a way that must have looked protective to outsiders. The women were chanting her name now, "Ka-te-ri-NA, Ka-te-ri-NA!" She saw the sea of applauding, chanting women even as Alex drew her away from the podium and through the door into the back. He was talking to his wrist as he hurried her across the wide dim room. Before she even realized it, he had hustled her out the back door, just as the limo pulled to a jerky stop. He opened the door, eased her into the back seat, climbed in beside her and slammed the door. "Go!" They were speeding away when the mob of reporters came surging around the building toward them.

"Dammit, dammit, *dammit,* woman."

"What?" she asked, though she knew perfectly well what.

"Do you have any idea what you have done?"

"It was bull, Alex. You guys had me reading utter bull."

"Maybe to you. But it was exactly what Katerina Barde planned to say at that luncheon."

"Then Katerina Barde doesn't have the ovaries to say what she really thinks. No intelligent woman could swallow that crap. Especially not one who practically grew up in the States."

He shook his head. From the front seat, Wes asked, "What happened? What did she do?"

"She started a second revolution in the country she's supposed to be protecting."

"Oh," Wes said. "Is that all?"

"Isn't that enough?"

"You're overreacting, Alex. Wes, all I did was say it was high time the women in this Tantilla place were treated with some dignity. Do you know they aren't allowed to drive or own property—or vote? Here I was reading this horsccrap that said we hoped that in five years we'd let them have licenses. Give 'em freaking tanks, instead. Then see who tells 'em they can't vote."

Wes slapped his knee and laughed out loud.

"Don't encourage her," Alex said. He turned to Mel. "You need to be clear on this. All those thoughts and convictions may be perfectly valid, but they are not Katerina's thoughts and convictions. They're yours. If you can't keep the two separate, you're going to blow this thing."

"Hell, I probably did them a favor."

He sighed. "If the wrong people pick up on the fact that you are not who you claim to be, you could get Katerina and Thomas killed. And that's no favor."

She was going to shoot back a scathing reply, but she couldn't come up with one. Instead she sighed, lowering her head. "You really think I might have given us away?"

"I don't know what to think."

"I'm sorry, Alex. I don't want to get anyone hurt, much less killed. I...look, I'll try harder, okay?"

"We're going to have to do better than this. A lot better."

She nodded in agreement, but she wasn't sure she could do much better than she was doing already.

In her royal chambers, the "princess" sat on the floor, surrounded by her royal subjects. She wore blue jeans and a black ribbed tank top that had a red skull and crossbones on the front, above the words "I bite." The bottom of the top didn't quite meet the waistband of the jeans. Her feet were bare, her face was scrubbed of any hint of makeup, and her hair was washed free of all the mousse and spray, towel dried and left to fall into its familiar short and riotous mess.

Vidalia sat in the rocking chair, her maid's uniform rumpled. Kara and Selene sat on the floor to either side of Mel. In the middle were a big chalk board, several pieces of chalk, a pair of erasers and a bowl of popcorn. In front of them, the widescreen TV flicked between clips of "Katerina's" speech, which had aired live in Tantilla via satellite, and shots of women protesting none too peacefully in the streets. The protests in Tantilla had sprung up within hours of the broadcast. Streets were blocked to traffic by angry women with signs and pictures of Katerina. Commerce had ground to a halt in the cities. Women were being arrested in droves, but the news channels reported that most were being released as soon as their husbands came to pick them up.

Alex was out, of course. He had a lot to answer for, after all.

Mel wrote on the board: Alex is going to *kill* me.

Selene smiled softly and shook her head side to side.

Kara took the board and wrote: Is he in very much trouble?

Mel shrugged.

Selene wrote: This is going to be a *good* thing, in the long run. She pointed to the women on the TV screen and wrote two more words: For them.

Mel took the board back and wrote: But not for me!

Muttering under her breath, Vidalia whispered. "Oh, for heaven's sakes, what are they gonna do, arrest you?"

Everyone shushed her at the same time, so it sounded like a tire had sprung a leak in the bedroom suite.

"Ridiculous," Vidalia said.

Selene spoke aloud. "Those women in Tantilla already loved and admired their Princess Katerina. Her words were all it took to convince them that they deserved better treatment. You spoke to them, and you empowered them. You have given them a hero. And I am proud to be your…housekeeper."

"Me, too!" Kara added with emphasis.

"Yeah, yeah, and I'm just over the moon to be your cook. Although with all the socializing you do, I'm afraid there's not much cooking to be done."

"The popcorn's great," Mel said, in an effort to placate her mother.

"Bah." She headed out of the room in a huff. The other three giggled when she left.

They continued watching the news, which cut to a live report from Tantilla, where President Belisle was about to give a news conference. He appeared on the screen, called for calm, asked the women of his nation to be patient and promised them that everything his daughter had said today was being taken under careful consideration.

"Think he means it?" Kara asked.

Mel shrugged. "I don't know. Maybe."

"He may not mean it now," Selene put in. "But the genie's out of the bottle. She's not going to go back in without a fight."

"And I pulled the cork," Mel said. She closed her eyes and silently cursed her temper.

Alex entered the room, took in the scene and seemed alarmed until he spotted the chalkboard. Mel stayed seated, while the other girls got to their feet quickly and hurried out of the room without a word. He just looked at her, and Mel continued to sit where she was and wondered just how angry he was right now.

He had been prepared to rip her to shreds for what she'd done, the second he could get her alone to do so. So why wasn't he?

Instead, he was looking at her sitting on the floor with her legs stretched out in front of her crossed at the ankles, leaning back on her elbows. The jeans suited her. The top, the strip of flesh between it and the jeans, the long, bare arms and shoulders…and her feet. She had the cutest feet.

Looking at her there, he saw a feisty, hot-tempered, ill-mannered, impatient, impulsive, passionate and surprisingly sexy woman. He liked the tint of her lips, a tea rose color, moist and pretty without being lined and darkened. He liked her eyes, which were fully dramatic enough without help from makeup. That color, like backlit sapphires, those thick dark lashes, didn't need enhancement. He liked her hair undone, because it looked as if someone had just run his hands through it. And he liked her face clean, because he could read it better. The way it paled when she was afraid, or colored when she was embarrassed or angry.

She was staring back at him with those big eyes, looking him over just as thoroughly. "I hope," she said, in character, "that my impulsive statements of today didn't cause trouble for you. That was never my intent."

"It wasn't your place," he told her. "You are not the president or even an elected official, and the things you said threw our country into turmoil."

"You're still angry."

"I'm trying to be. I took a lot of heat for you today."

She sighed. "I'd gladly have taken it myself."

He met her eyes, got a little bit lost in their fire. "I don't doubt that."

"I spoke from the heart. And you know as well as I do that every word I said was true and right."

He blinked, unable to argue with that. "Change takes time."

"It seemed to me, at that moment, that I didn't have time."

What was she saying? "Katerina, your mission here is not to change the world."

"No. But if I change one little corner of the world in the process, then where's the harm?"

He closed his eyes. "The president—your father—is furious."

"His daughter isn't."

He almost asked her how she could know that, but bit his lip in time.

"Can we go away, Thomas? For a walk somewhere private? A park or—"

He turned away quickly. "There's no time. We have a state dinner at the mayor's mansion."

She sighed, got to her feet and looked at the closetful of clothes she hated, and he could see that she was dreading the thought of getting back into costume again.

"Afterward we'll have time," he promised.

She shot him a grateful look. "Thank you."

He nodded and left her to get ready.

Mel sat stiffly at the long, elegant table, draped in a pristine white, lace-trimmed cloth. The plates were heavy, even when nothing was on them, and they were edged in what she assumed was a thick band of real gold. Silver candlesticks, each holding a single white taper, stood in a row every foot or so along the center. The flames reflected on all the silverware, the spotless glasses and the wine they held.

Like children at their first mixed-gender party, the guests had been seated boy, girl, boy, girl. The women at the table were all perfectly poised, comfortable in their hair and makeup, wearing the latest designer fashions. They moved and spoke and acted their parts so much more naturally than Mel could hope to do. Their manners were second nature. They were smart and witty and charming.

She felt like a stray mongrel junkyard dog at a table of pedigreed poodles.

"We were all very surprised by your comments at the luncheon today, Ms. Barde," said a senator's wife, who looked like a supermodel and spoke in a smooth Texas drawl, slight enough to make her seem even more attractive. "Whatever made you do such an impulsive thing?"

Mel shrugged. "What makes you think it wasn't planned?"

The other woman blinked. "Well, I…it was obvious the way you just seemed to toss the prepared speech aside, calling it…what you did."

"My wife is growing proficient at adding theatrical twists to her public appearances," Alex said smoothly. "And it did have the desired results."

"Sheer brilliance," another woman said. "I knew it all the time, of course."

The first one was eyeing her still.

"You really don't sound foreign at all."

"I was educated here in the States from the time I was thirteen," Mel said in Katerina's slow, gentle way. "Some even say they detect a hint of Southern accent in my voice from time to time. Which doesn't surprise me. I did spend a lot of time in the South."

"Really? Where?"

Mel lowered her head. "Must we spend the entire evening talking about me?"

"You *are* the guest of honor."

Alex patted her hand from beside her. "Try to smile through it, love, as you tell the same old stories for the ten-thousandth time. It's your duty to entertain your dinner companions."

"Here, now," the mayor said from a few seats down. "If anything, it's our duty to entertain the two of you! Enough with the questions."

The rest of the evening passed slowly, but at least bearably, as she was required to speak very little. She nearly freaked when the first course was served, and she glanced down at the overabundance of silverware flanking her plate. But Alex was quick. Nothing got past the man. He caught her eye, picked up the appropriate fork, and she remembered Bernadette's instructions that one always used the silver on the outside first.

It was only afterward, in the limo on the way back, that she realized she had survived the evening without any major disasters.

"You can relax now," Alex said as they rode in the limo back to their temporary home.

"Speak for yourself."

"You did fine, Mel."

"Meaning that I didn't create an international incident over dessert?"

"Meaning that you were convincing in your role. Perhaps a little less friendly than Katerina would have been, but—"

"Friendly? You expected me to be friendly to those phoney baloney rich bitches?"

He blinked as if she'd struck him. "You have something against rich people?" he asked. "Don't forget, your sister married one."

She crossed her arms and huffed. He studied her. "I thought they were perfectly polite to you. What is your problem?"

"Were we even at the same table?"

"As far as I know."

"Look, that one with the big red hair is sleeping with the short guy."

He blinked and gave his head a shake.

"And the two blondes were taking potshots at each other all night long, and all the mayor's wife kept doing was try to make sure everyone knew this was *her* party, and that creepy senator guy was hitting on me all night."

"He was *what?*"

"Oh, come on, you didn't notice? And here I was thinking you didn't miss a thing."

"If I had noticed, I'd have damn well done something about it!" He seemed surprised by the decibel level of his own voice. When he spoke again, it was much more quietly. "Thomas wouldn't take something like that very well, so I'd have to reflect his reactions."

"Oh. So what do you suppose wimpy little Katerina would have done to that political groupie who was eyeing you like a juicy steak?"

"I don't know what you're talking about."

"The one who invited herself to stop in for a visit tomorrow."

"Mel, that woman is a Federal judge."

"She's a slut, and she's after my man."

A slow smile spread over his face. "Oh, really?"

"Well, that's the way Katerina would see it. And I should react accordingly."

"You two are freakin' pathetic," Wes said from the front seat.

"You're lucky I didn't get up and pop her in the nose," Mel said, ignoring him.

Alex closed his eyes.

"What?" she asked.

"I'm just imagining the scandal that would erupt if a foreign dignitary had punched a Federal judge over a state dinner. Good God. You've got to get yourself under control, Mel. Katerina is not impulsive or hot-tempered or jealous, so you can't be, either."

"Who the hell said I was jealous?"

There was a loud pop, just before the car veered sideways into a skid. Mel slammed into Alex's chest, and he quickly held her there, pressing her down with one

hand and pulling out his gun with the other. Wes grap-
pled with the wheel. The car's back end jerked from
side to side like the tail of an agitated cat, before the
vehicle finally came to a stop on the shoulder of the
road in a cloud of dust and darkness.

"What the hell was that?" Mel asked, as she started
to sit up.

Alex's hand was still on her back, and he held her
down. "Stay put."

"But—"

"Just in case," he said, his tone gentler. "It was
probably just a blowout, but we need to make sure.
Okay?"

Looking up at him, she nodded once. Alex glanced
into the front seat. "Wes, are you armed?"

"Damn straight I am." Wes lifted his hand slightly,
and Mel saw the big revolver he held.

"Watch her. Anybody besides me gets near this car,
take her the hell out of here as fast as you can go. If
you have to shoot, shoot. Save the second-guessing for
later. Can you do that?"

"Not only can I, but I've had to prove it a time or
two. Go ahead."

"Go?" Mel asked. "Go where?"

"I need to get out, take a look around, check the
tire." He glanced at Wes again, maybe to tell him to
call for backup, but Wes was already putting the mobile
phone to his ear. So he opened his door and got out,
gun ready.

Mel peered out the limo window from a low position
and watched his every move, terrified something was
going to happen to him. He looked up and down the
road, scanned the bushes along the roadside, beyond the
ditch, but Mel doubted there was anything to be seen.

Minimal lighting, full dark outside, he'd be lucky if he could see a freaking hit squad if they were determined to stay hidden. He made the effort all the same, and she noticed he kept one eye on the car the entire time.

"Was that a gunshot, Wes?" she asked, as she watched Alex.

"I don't know. It could have been."

"Shouldn't he be in here, waiting for help to arrive?"

"It's not in his nature to sit and wait."

"No, it's in his nature to parade around out there like a great big target."

Wes shook his head. "It's in his nature to put himself between the shooter and his intended target."

"That's bull. That only applies if the intended target is some VIP he's been assigned to protect. I'm nothing. I'm a prop."

"Oh, I think he'd disagree with you there."

She looked over the seat at Wes, but he averted his eyes.

Finally Alex gave up and came back to the vehicle, then bent to take a look at the tire.

Mel heard sirens. The cavalry had arrived.

Alex noticed that Mel took her time in the tub that night. There wasn't much he didn't notice about her. He imagined she was soaking away every hint of the woman she seemed to be getting so sick and tired of. She flat-out refused to wear the frilly white nightgown Bernadette had left out for her. Instead, she walked into the living room of the suite wearing a hockey jersey and a pair of ankle socks. White ones. She'd towel dried her hair and washed off all her makeup.

Alex sat on that small settee, tired to the bone. He'd peeled off the fake coat of whiskers. He had a decent start on some real ones underneath it, and he hoped they would grow in quickly enough that he could stop wearing the phony beard. Mel walked to the settee, sat down beside him. He guessed she must want to talk to him, and she couldn't do that from a chair across the room.

He had loosened his tie, and the top button of his shirt was undone. His hair was less than neat. Combined with the unshaven face, he figured he probably looked pretty bad to her. Certainly less like the man she had referred to as a *GQ* P.I.

He was watching the late news. They were showing clips of Mel's speech today, and then a still shot of the limo as its tire was being changed on the side of the road. The two of them had been long gone by the time that shot had been taken. The cops had hauled them both back here quick as a flash. Nobody wanted the beloved princess killed on his watch.

Alex studied her as she sat there beside him. He picked up the remote without looking away from her, thumbed the volume button until the television was far too loud and whispered, "You all right?"

"That depends," she whispered back. "Was it a blowout or a gunshot we heard tonight?"

Alex thought about lying to her. Would have, if she had been anyone else. But she wasn't. She was tough enough to handle the truth, and sharp enough to know it when she heard it. "I couldn't tell by looking. We should have an answer by morning, though."

"I don't understand what the point would be in someone shooting out our tire."

He shrugged. "They might not have been aiming for the tire."

She held his eyes with hers for a moment. A creature with eyes like hers ought to be timid, he thought. Shy and easily frightened. Doe eyes. She didn't act like a doe. She held his gaze without blinking and said, "I want a gun."

A flat-out no jumped to his lips, but he didn't let it out. She wasn't any ordinary woman. He could tell her there was no need, and she would just counter, that if there were no need, he wouldn't be carrying one. Nor would the Secret Service agents assigned to her, nor would Wes. There was no point in pretense with her. No need for it, either. "Have you ever fired one?"

She nodded. "I live in the country. I'd never been without a gun until the twins were born."

"What are you used to?"

"A twenty-gauge shotgun," she said, "but I suppose that would look a little conspicuous. I can handle a revolver. I've never fired a semiautomatic like you're carrying, and I think I prefer not to. So a revolver."

"It'll have to be small enough to carry concealed. I'll get you something tomorrow."

"A snub-nosed thirty-eight will be just fine. Don't go bringing me some dainty little twenty-two. If I have to shoot someone, I want to do some damage."

"Understood."

She nodded once, lowered her eyes. "That scared the hell out of me."

"Me, too."

"You're not supposed to get scared."

"The only people who don't get scared are already dead."

She smiled a little. "Literally or figuratively?"

"Either. Maybe both."

Drawing a slow breath, she got to her feet. "I'm exhausted." Then, with a glance toward the bedroom, she asked, "So how are we doing this?"

He stood up, too, closing the distance between them so he could keep his voice low. "As convincingly as possible." He flicked the off button on the remote, dropped it onto the sofa, slipped back into his Thomas persona. "Go on to bed, my darling. I promise I won't be long."

She rolled her eyes, but she did go into the bedroom.

Alex tugged his tie the rest of the way off and unbuttoned his shirt on the way to the shower. He told himself he would have no problem sleeping with Melusine all night and behaving like a man of class and breeding.

Chapter 5

Mel crawled into the giant bed, burrowed beneath its mounds of covers and felt comforted by the softness surrounding her. Not as much as she would have in her own bed, beneath her own covers, but she supposed a little comfort was better than none. She could hear the shower running. Alex was in there right now. Probably naked.

She didn't suppose he *slept* naked. He was far too civilized for that. And even if he did, he wouldn't try it here. He probably had a pair of expensive silk pajamas or something.

The bed was certainly big enough. So big she probably wouldn't even notice a difference when he got in. Maybe she could manage to fall asleep before then. That would probably be a good idea.

She closed her eyes, curled onto her side, tried to relax her face.

The shower stopped running. She tried to tune out

the sounds of Alex moving around the bathroom, toweling down, padding around in his bare feet. She wasn't having much luck.

The bathroom door opened. She had turned off the bedroom light, and he stumbled in the darkness. Something tipped over. He swore softly.

"Are you all right?" she asked. "I'm sorry, I should have left the light on."

"It's all right, no harm done." He said it in his accented voice, reminding her that, even now, they might not be alone. He righted whatever he had knocked down, then crossed to the bed and slid beneath the covers. She went stiff as a board when his body cuddled up to hers and his arm came around her.

"What are you…?"

His whiskery cheek rasped her neck, and she shivered as he whispered into her ear. Such a delicious sensation rippled through her that it was a moment before she realized what he was saying.

"There was a tiny camera in the clock on the bedside stand," he whispered. Then his lips brushed her neck, and her breath stuttered out of her. "I found it when I knocked the clock over. It was aimed at the bed."

"Move it, then," she whispered.

"Did. But there could be others."

She rolled onto her back, because she couldn't bear those whiskers on her neck, or those lips brushing her skin and her ear, another moment. But that was a mistake, because now she had to look into his eyes. It was dark, but not pitch-dark. She could see him, could see the way he was staring down at her. He lay on his side, his face only inches from hers. He brushed her hair away from her face with one lazy hand.

She rubbed her cheek against his, feeling the rasp of

his whiskers like the most sinful touch she could imagine. Then she reminded herself she was only doing it to get close enough to whisper into his ear, "So just how far do we need to take this charade, Alex?"

"Only from the neck up," he muttered into her ear, nibbling it a little in the process. "Think you can handle that?"

"I can if you can." She pulled her cheek across his one last time, then looked into his eyes. They were lying on their sides, facing each other. He slid his arm around her waist and pressed his mouth to hers.

Mel was surprised that he went so far as to actually kiss her. But she was even more surprised by the rush of feeling that shot through her when his warm, soft lips pressed against hers, and she felt her own lips move in some unplanned, almost instinctive response. His arm tightened around her waist, pulling her body closer to his. Her hand slid to the back of his head, fingers in his hair. His mouth was pressing, sliding, against hers, and hers against his. She was never sure whose lips parted first, whose tongue was the first to join in the game. It happened so naturally that she couldn't determine when the kiss changed from a staged portrayal to a real one. But there was no question that it did. Her body heated, and her heart pounded. She pressed closer to him, and he held her closer still, and their mouths fed from each other. Her hands tangled in his hair to pull him closer, and his hand slid beneath her body, her waist, her buttocks. Oh, no, he was pressing against her, and he was hard, and she could feel him....

Alex suddenly broke the kiss. He was panting. So was she. Their bodies were still melded from chest to thigh, arms still locked around each other. Her eyes wide, searching his, she whispered, "What the hell just happened?"

He pressed a hand to the back of her head, pulled her closer, so her face nestled in the crook of his neck even as he rolled onto his back. "Nothing. It was nothing. Just a kiss." He was breathless when he said it.

"Yeah, like I'm just a princess."

"Go to sleep," he whispered.

"You think I'm going to *sleep* after that?" Beneath her head, his heart was thumping hard. "I thought you didn't like me."

"So did I. Now go to sleep."

She sighed, snuggled close to him, her head remaining where it was and his arm remaining lightly around her. It was interesting, this new twist things had taken. She lay there wide awake, turning it over in her mind. And over, and over, and over.

Alex lay on his back, feigning sleep, while his brain shot questions like fireworks. He liked Melusine Brand; he had already known that. He liked her honesty. Her lack of pretense. The countless ways in which she differed from the other women he had known. But he wasn't attracted to her. Okay, he was. A little. To the same degree any straight, relatively sane male would be attracted to a beautiful woman like Mel. But nothing beyond that. Or at least he hadn't thought so.

Now, though, he was worried.

She lay close to him, her head resting on his shoulder and chest, so that her hair was under his nose and its scent wafted up to him with every breath he took. She was warm in his arms, and so close. He liked the way it felt to hold her.

He tried to recall liking the way it felt to just hold a

woman, but he didn't think it was something he'd experienced before. He told himself he must have. But if he had, he couldn't recall it to mind now. He could remember enjoying a film with a woman, enjoying a dance, enjoying witty conversation about subjects that interested him. Sex, certainly he always enjoyed sex.

But this…this…cuddling?

She sighed softly and burrowed closer.

Oddly, the other thing he enjoyed most with her was the way she argued with him—her unpolished, straightforward reactions and her talent at bantering.

He didn't sleep all night. By morning his head ached, probably from the nightlong internal dialogue going on inside it. His back ached from trying so hard to lie still, because God forbid she wake up and move into an even more intimate position.

He didn't move until she stirred awake. She woke like a kitten, stretching and making little purring sounds. Then her head lifted from his chest, and she blinked sleepily down at him.

But that dopey, sexy, sleepy smile died slowly as she looked into his eyes, and when he said, "Good morning," her reply was, "Oh, my God, I just figured it out."

"Just figured what out, *Katerina?*" He put as much emphasis as he could on the name, to remind her of her role and of those who might be listening in.

She narrowed her eyes. "Exactly." Then she rolled away from him and got out the other side of the bed. Her strides were long, her footfalls angry. And he wondered just what he had done to offend her.

She opened the doors to the walk-in closet and vanished into its depths. When she came out again, muttering, she was carrying a pretty, feminine, mint-green suit by its hanger. She tugged open a dresser drawer and yanked out silky undergarments and nylons. Then she went into the bathroom and slammed the door.

Alex felt as if a tornado had just spun through the room.

Okay, okay, obviously he'd pissed her off. She hadn't fallen asleep angry, but she had certainly awoken that way. He had to find out why. Not that it mattered in the least or had any bearing on the job they were here to do. But he had to know, nonetheless. And he certainly wasn't going to find out here.

She couldn't talk to him here, even if she wanted to. Maybe she didn't want to.

Sighing, he got out of bed. Standing up made the headache considerably worse, but he had no choice. He was careful to keep his head down, so as not to reveal his lack of a beard to any prying eyes or lenses, though the room was still dim. There were things to do, arrangements to be made. There was the ball tonight. Good God, the ball. What a fiasco that was going to be. He wondered belatedly if Mel could even dance.

Going to his own closet, he removed a suit, chose a tie. He intended to go to one of the guest rooms to shower and dress, but just as he reached the door, he paused, set the clothes down and returned to the bedroom. The shower was still running in the bathroom. He doubted it would do anything to cool her temper. He knew her temper. If she was angry, she would stay angry until and unless she was given a reason not to be. He didn't want her angry with him today. It could blow the entire game.

He took a sheet of stationery from the drawer of the writing desk and stood with the pen poised above it for a full minute, before he forcibly swallowed his pride and wrote, "You were right. It wasn't just a kiss." He gave a nod, certain it had been that comment of his that must have angered and offended her. Folding the note in two, he left it on the bed.

An hour later he sat at the large breakfast table, waiting for her to put in an appearance. He'd been there twenty minutes already, and he had a dozen things to do, but for some reason he didn't want to leave until he'd seen her this morning.

When she finally arrived in the breakfast room she was in full Princess Katerina mode. The suit was feminine and yet utterly dignified all at once. Mint-green skirt that came just to the knee, a pearl silk blouse with a lace collar, and a beaded belt knotted at her waist, its long ends dangling. The earrings matched the belt, only tinier. Her makeup was flawless, her hair sprayed even more stiffly than usual. Her shoes matched her blouse, and her smile was frozen in place.

He rose when she came to the table, met her halfway and kissed her hand. "Good morning, love."

She met his eyes. He searched hers, looking for some sign of her mood. But there was nothing there. No hint of Mel at all. Nothing but Katerina. "Good morning, Thomas."

She took her seat, and he took his, across from her. He didn't know if she had found the note, or what she thought about it if she had. He didn't know if she was still angry. He didn't know anything. When her mother came out with the silver pot to fill her cup, Mel called her "Vi" and asked how she was this morning. She chattered in that soft cheerful tone, in a pitch higher than her own, and tones that were gentler and more refined, about the weather and the coffee until Alex could have happily strangled her.

Vidalia looked at her, frowning, then shot Alex a questioning glance. Alex could only shrug. He had no idea when or why Mel had decided to embrace her persona so devotedly. He supposed it was a good thing. But he didn't like it.

"Are you looking forward to the ball tonight?" he asked her, partly because there was a lull in the conversation and partly because he was hoping to see a brief glimpse of Mel behind the Katerina facade.

"I can hardly wait," she replied, quickly and easily. "Wait until you see my dress."

Right. Mel Brand excited about a ball gown. He knew better. Exasperated, he pushed away from the table and got to his feet, and crossing the room made a quick call to the driver's quarters.

"You're leaving?"

"I have a few errands to run. Will you walk with me to the car, love?"

"Of course." She got up, too, and walked with him, placing her feet just so, keeping her posture impeccable and her smile ever in place. When they got to the front door and stepped out, she looked around, but the limo wasn't waiting. "Didn't you call ahead?"

"I told him to give us a few minutes." He walked her farther from the house, out into the driveway, into the open. "Now, keep in mind there are surveillance cameras—"

"Aren't there always?" she asked from behind the fake smile.

"But we can speak freely out here, within reason."

"About what?"

"About us. About last night, and…and this morning. What did I do to make you so angry?"

"Don't be silly, darling. Katerina Barde doesn't get angry."

"No, but Melusine Brand does—and did. What I want to know is, why?"

She blinked. A tiny ripple in the mask's perfection. She looked away from him. "It really doesn't matter."

"It does matter. Were you offended because I kissed you? Or because I stopped?"

Her gaze shot to his again. "You didn't kiss *me* at all. You kissed Katerina."

He frowned, completely confused. "Look, did you even get the note I left?"

"I got it."

"Well?"

"Well what?"

He sighed, looking skyward as if for help. "I apologize for saying it was just a kiss last night, that it didn't mean anything. It's obvious there's something— some...chemistry or something—between us, and it was callous of me to say there wasn't." He searched her eyes, but there was no sign she was getting his point. "It's just that this is no time to be...distracted by it, whatever it was. And beyond that, I was taken by surprise. Weren't you?"

"I was. Until I realized that you were right. It was nothing. There *is* no 'chemistry,' as you call it, between you and me." She turned away.

He caught her shoulder, turned her back to face him. "No? Then what was that last night?"

"I thought you just said this was no time to be distracted by it?"

"Oh, come on, Mel. At least tell me what you think happened last night."

She shrugged delicately. "I haven't got a clue. *That*

was between you and Katerina. I had nothing to do with it.''

''Huh?''

The limo came creeping along the drive, so they had to move out of its way. The window came down slowly. ''You ready, boss?'' Wes called.

Alex held up a hand for patience. ''Mel, you've got to tell me what you're getting at here. Call me dense, but you're not making any sense.''

''Fine, I'll explain it to you very quickly and very simply. I am not Katerina Barde. I am not a woman who dresses the way I'm dressed or speaks the way I'm speaking. I don't have manners or breeding, and I detest tact. It's a cop-out. I don't like makeup or high heels or hair spray. None of this is who I am. You know that. You've been around me before, and you never felt the slightest inclination to kiss me then. The person you feel attracted to is make-believe. She's not real. And even if she were, she's certainly not me.''

She turned on her heel and walked back into the house.

His head reeling, Alex got into the limo and closed the door.

Wes looked at him in the rearview mirror. ''You look like you've been hit between the eyes with a mallet.''

''Feel like it, too.''

''Mel?''

''Yes.'' He glanced up, startled.

''Don't worry,'' Wes said. ''I had them sweep the car just before I pulled it out of the garage this morning. It's clean.''

''You're not bad at this cloak-and-dagger stuff, for a cowboy,'' Alex said.

''My brother's a lawman. You pick it up.'' He drove

to the gates, which opened, and the limo rolled through them. "So Mel's pissed at you, I take it?"

"She's pretty angry."

"What did you do?"

"I, uh, I kissed her."

"Oh. Did she like it?"

"I thought so at the time."

"Hmm. Women. Who the hell can figure them out?"

"I wish to God I knew."

"Hey, we could call in reinforcements. My baby sister, Jessi, would probably be able to interpret it over the phone, for Pete's sake."

"No." Alex wondered why he had even spoken to Wes Brand about any of this. "We aren't going to risk a mission this important over your irrational cousin's latest tantrum."

Wes nodded slowly. "Well, then you might want to try talking to Selene or Kara. But not Vidalia. Good God, if she knew you'd kissed her daughter and then spent the night in the same bedroom, she'd like to skin you alive."

"It's difficult speaking freely in the house."

"Then get out of the house," Wes suggested.

It was, Alex thought, a good suggestion. Not the talking to Mel's sisters part, but the part about getting out of the house. Maybe Mel just needed a break.

Wes drove Alex Stone to the Federal Building, then waited an hour to drive him back to the pretentious mansion again. He hadn't quite gotten a handle on the fellow yet. At first he hadn't expected to like him at all. But then something had struck him as clear and familiar, easily recognizable to Wes, who'd seen it often before. The man had a core in him that was solid. He was honest. And he was determined to protect Mel from any harm. Those were qualities you couldn't fake. Not to the discerning eyes of a Brand, anyway. He knew a man when he met one, and the more time he spent with Alex Stone, the more convinced Wes was that he was just that. A man.

A man who was rapidly falling for a Brand woman. That wasn't something Wes thought would be pleasant, or easy, for any man. Even one as decent as Stone.

He dropped Alex at the front door, watched him in, then drove the limo around the house to the garage. After he put the car in, secured the garage and pocketed the keys and alarm control, he went in through the back entrance to the kitchen, where, just as expected, he found Selene.

The youngest of the Oklahoma litter, she was stunning to look at. Hair such a pale blond it appeared silver, and those pale-blue eyes that reminded him of an Arctic wolf. There was something about this little cousin of his. He'd never noticed it when he'd been a child, those few times his family had interacted with hers. Of course, back then he hadn't been what he was now.

She turned from the counter where she'd been chopping vegetables and sent him a knowing smile. "Hello, Wes. I've been hoping for a private conversation with you. Coffee?"

"Got anything colder?"

She nodded toward the refrigerator. "Help yourself." She picked up the cutting board, used the knife to push all the vegetables from it into the pot bubbling on the stove. Then she moved to the sink to rinse the board, the knife, and her hands.

Wes took a soft drink from the fridge, glancing at her as she wiped her hands on a towel. "One for you?"

"Yes, thanks."

He grabbed her a cola, handed it to her, then went to the kitchen door to open it, and let her precede him outside. He didn't need to tell her they couldn't speak freely in the house. Not even in the kitchen. They had all been briefed.

They walked along the narrow white gravel path that twisted from the house out into the gardens in the back. He sipped his soft drink, and she sipped hers, and he wondered who was going to start. Finally she glanced up at him and asked, "So why are you really here?"

He didn't bother pretending. Not with this girl. She knew, and he knew that she knew. "I had a dream," he said. "I dreamed about your sister. Even though I hadn't seen any of you in well over a decade, I dreamed about her."

"What did you dream?"

He pursed his lips. "She was here, in Austin. And she was in danger." He shook his head. "I know it's all pretty vague, but that's honestly all I got. I saw her in my mind, and she looked scared. She was in the dark, but I knew she was in Austin. When I woke, a wolf was crying outside my window."

"And that was significant to you?"

He nodded. "I'm a Shaman, Selene. Wolf is my totem. When he tells me something is important, I pay attention. So I looked up the number and called your mother in Big Falls. Asked her if any of her daughters were going to be in Austin. She said no, but a couple of days later, she called me back."

"Right after Alex showed up asking Mel to take part in this ruse."

He nodded.

Selene licked her lips. "Right after Alex told us what he wanted Mel to do, I got this horrible feeling about it. Then, all that night, I felt this foreboding, like a dark shadow hanging over all of us, waiting to fall. I got up, took out my Tarot cards."

She looked at him, waiting, he thought, for some kind of comment.

"I knew you were a seer," he said.

"More than a seer, but that's beside the point. The cards that fell were not good. Something is going to happen. I just wish I knew what, or when, but I'm drawing a blank."

"Me, too."

She drew a breath, closed her hand around his. "I'm really glad you're here, cousin."

"A family reunion is long overdue. When we get through this mess, we really need to do something about rebuilding those old ties, don't you think?"

"Whatever rift there was between us, it's so old that I don't see how it could matter anymore," Selene said.

"Oh, it matters. To your mother, especially. My branch of the family hurt her pretty badly a long time ago. But I think we can heal that wound now."

"Hey, how can we fail, with two magical people in the family?"

"Three. Ben studied Buddhism with a Zen master from Tibet. He's pretty amazing."

"I never would have guessed."

He studied her face for a long moment. "What's your calling, Selene?"

She lowered her eyes, shook her head. "I'm not ready to talk about it yet."

"You can trust me, you know. I won't judge you."

"Mamma will. This isn't the time."

"All right."

She drew a nasal breath, looked around at the gardens, the late-blooming flowers and the shrubs. "Thanks for being here, Wes. It means a lot to me. To all of us."

"It's not just me, kiddo. The rest of the family is only a phone call away. They don't know what's going on—well, except for Garrett—but they'll be here in a heartbeat if we need them."

She smiled. "Sounds just like our family."

"We *are* your family." He lifted his brows. "And I've got pictures!" He located a bench in the garden, and they went to sit down while Wes tugged out his wallet and began flipping through the small photos. "Here's my wife, Taylor, and our little baby boy. He's just six months old. His native name is Wolf."

Selene's eyes sparkled as she looked at the photo. "That's a story you're going to have to tell me sometime soon."

"I will. Maybe around a bonfire one night with both families gathered." He nodded firmly, setting that goal in his mind. "My son's English name is Jonathon Orrin Brand."

Selene blinked and looked up from the photo. "Jonathon was my father's name."

"And Orrin was my father's. They were brothers, and they were estranged. But they're both gone now, and we need to start again. I was thinking about that long rift in the family when Taylor and I chose Jonathon's name."

Selene put her arms around his neck and hugged him gently. When she straightened away, she was misty-eyed and sniffling.

"We'd, uh, best get back to the house. Be nearby in case they need us," Wes said. But deep down, he felt like he'd found a long-lost baby sister.

Selene nodded and got to her feet. "You go on ahead. I want to gather some weeds before that pesky gardener gets out here and ruins them again." He arched a brow. "Nettle, burdock and dandelion," she said. "They're very protective."

He nodded, glanced around the area, and decided it wasn't good to leave her alone. There were plenty of agents in the house to protect Mel and Alex, but no one in sight of the garden out here. So he remained on the bench. "I'll wait."

"What did you find out, dear?" Mel asked in her best Katerina voice. She'd been waiting in the foyer for Alex's return, largely because there was little else for her to do. Thank-you cards needed to go out, but they had a forger on hand who was far better at copying Katerina's handwriting than Mel would ever be, so he was taking care of that little job. And there were no social events slated until the ball that night.

"What did I find out about what?" he asked, as if she were the airhead this prissy little voice made her sound like.

"About the blowout last night, on the limo? I assumed that was one of the errands you had to run this morning. Following up on what those nice policemen found when they ran their tests."

He shot her a look, and she knew she was piling the ditz routine on a bit. She wondered irritably if he knew the real Katerina. Had he been high on the woman already, long before Mel had taken on her role, or was this a new development?

''You assumed correctly,'' he said.

''Well? Tell me the truth, Thomas. Contrary to public perception, I'm not a fragile flower who will wilt at the slightest sign of trouble. Did the tire blow out on its own, or was that sound we heard what it sounded like?''

He licked his lips, studied her face and drew a deep breath. ''It was a gunshot.''

Chapter 6

She paled. Alex saw it clearly, but he had expected it. Contrary to her own opinion, he thought sarcastically, Melusine Brand was not made of stone. He was close enough to put his arm around her, and he did it automatically. It was only as he led her to a chair and eased her down onto it that he realized he was acting his role without meaning to. Without thinking about it.

"I'll get you a glass of water."

"No."

"Something stronger?"

She shook her head left, then right, and seemed to gather herself, to focus her vision. "I just never expected—I really expected you to say it was just a blowout." She lifted her gaze to lock it with his. "Someone *shot* at us?"

"Not necessarily."

She lifted her brows.

"It could have been an accident. They could have

been shooting at something or someone else, and we just got in the way of a stray bullet.''

''Oh, yeah. That's likely. Was it a high crime area we were driving through? A place where gangs hang out? Or maybe it was just hunting season on that particular stretch of highway.''

''Calm down, Katerina.''

Her eyes flashed wider and she whispered, ''Do you really think I'm going to continue this game when I'm being shot at? You told me this would be safe.''

''Steps are being taken—''

''Steps? They shot at us last night. Is this not registering in your brain somehow?''

He pursed his lips, reached into his pocket, took out the small revolver he'd acquired for her. ''As I promised,'' he told her, handing her the gun.

She flipped open the cylinder, checked to be sure it was loaded, clapped it shut again. She pointed it at something beyond the nearest window, her grip as good as his own. Her hands didn't even shake.

''I'll need more—''

He handed her the box of ammo before she could finish the sentence, telling her with his eyes to watch what she said aloud. ''We haven't found those two items we've been looking for yet,'' he told her softly. ''For the first time, we have to consider the possibility that they might have been...taken.''

''You mean...?'' She blinked in shock, and he could see by her eyes that she understood he was referring to Katerina and Thomas Barde. ''My God. This...this changes everything.''

''Yeah. It does.'' He licked his lips.

She got up from the chair suddenly, gripped his hand and tugged him behind her through the house, up the wide staircase to their suite, and through it, into the bathroom. Just as he had done before, she closed the door, then walked around turning on all the faucets, flipping on the fan. Steam billowed. The hot tub bubbled.

She turned to him, stood very close, so close he might have thought she was going to kiss him if he hadn't known better. He kept remembering last night. What it felt like to kiss her. To have her kiss him back. His heartbeat sped up, and his body tensed in reaction to the memory and to her closeness.

"Are you telling me that Katerina and Thomas have been kidnapped?" she whispered.

He averted his eyes. "We don't know that."

"But we have reason to think it, when it wasn't even considered before?"

He met her probing gaze. "Their limo and their driver have been found in the desert. They were apparently on their way here from whatever love-nest they'd been visiting when they were intercepted."

Staring into his eyes she whispered, "Their driver? Dead?"

He nodded. "We know it wasn't a simple robbery because his wallet was still on him, cash and plastic. And we know it was recent, as the driver had only been dead a matter of hours."

Her knees buckled, and Alex gripped her shoulders, helped her sit down on the edge of the oversize tub. "We can't be sure they were taken," he whispered. "They could have escaped, run off, gone into hiding."

"Oh, right. I'm sure the *princess* got a long way in her four-inch stilettos and designer gown in the desert." She shook her head. "No, they would have contacted someone if they'd escaped."

"Maybe the driver was killed after dropping the couple off somewhere. Maybe the killers still don't know where the couple are hiding."

"And we were shot at last night because...?"

"We can only guess at that. The current favorite theory is that the kidnappers have been monitoring the news. When they saw you and me and heard no mention of the Bardes being missing, they might have believed they'd been duped. Maybe they think they grabbed a pair of doubles, who were sent on ahead of the real couple as a security measure."

"So they think *we* are the real Katerina and Thomas?"

"It's possible. As I said, that's just the current pet theory."

"But wouldn't that put the others in danger?"

"The kidnappers would want to make sure first."

"And now they're after us."

"We can't be sure of that."

She lowered her head, licked her lips. "Look, no amount of money is worth getting killed for. I signed on for this with the understanding that it would be safe, that the real couple were just off on a lark somewhere."

"I know. And I'm getting you out of here just as soon as it can be arranged. We need to be sure it's safe, be sure you aren't followed when you leave here, and we have to come up with a plausible reason to tell the world why Katerina Barde has dropped out of sight."

She sighed. "And what about you?"

"I'm staying on in the role of Thomas."

Her eyes got wider, intense. Worried, he thought. For him? "Why on earth would you do that?" she asked. "Someone wants to *kill* Thomas."

"You're right. I think they would kill Thomas as

soon as look at him, then hold Katerina as leverage to wrest political control from her father. But if they think they might have the wrong couple, they won't do anything except try to verify who's who. The longer and more convincingly I can play this role, keep them uncertain, the longer the real Thomas gets to live."

She stared at him for a long moment. "I…I didn't realize…. I didn't think of that."

"There's no reason you *should* think of that. This isn't your problem, Mel. We're shipping your mom and sisters out today. No one would have any reason to be suspicious of staff leaving here, so they'll be safe. They're going to the Brand ranch in Quinn. That's near El Paso."

"I know where it is. Why aren't they just going home?"

"It's just a precaution. Just in case anyone uncovers your real identity and traces you back to Big Falls, Oklahoma. Your other two sisters and their families are already being moved to Quinn."

She nodded slowly. "What about Wes?" Those blue eyes dilated again. "He's our driver. They *killed* the other driver."

Alex nodded. "I know. He fought it, but we finally convinced him to escort your sisters and mother back to Quinn. He was bound and determined not to leave until you did. I had a hell of a job convincing him he could trust me to keep you safe for a few hours."

"I'm surprised you were able to convince him at all."

Alex averted his eyes, not wanting to tell her any details about his conversation with Wes. He'd had to admit some things he would rather not bring up again just now.

"So that's where I'll be going there, too?" she asked. "The Texas Brand in Quinn?"

Sighing, he sat down on the tub's edge beside her. "Yes. Just as soon as we get everything in place. They'll be expecting the two of us at that ball tonight. Not showing would tip them off immediately. So we will arrive, but you won't be staying. It'll be crowded, confusing. The perfect time for us to spirit you away. I'll keep their attention on me while some other agents whisk you out of there. No one will realize you're gone until the end of the evening, when the place clears out. If I play it right, it'll look as if the two of us slipped away together, went home before the end of the evening and straight to bed. With any luck they won't know you're gone until tomorrow."

"Just who are 'they,' Alex?"

"The CIA thinks it's Curnyn Shaw. They've been in touch with President Belisle to bring him up to speed."

"He'll probably break off all relations with the U.S. over this," Mel said.

"Not until his daughter's rescued. He needs to work with us. After that—well, I think a lot depends on how all this turns out."

She licked her lips, turned her head, met his eyes. "Things sound pretty grim, don't they?"

He nodded.

"I, um, I want to say goodbye to my family before they leave."

"Of course." He ran a hand over the back of her hair, crown to nape. "I'm sorry I got you into this, Melusine. I honestly thought it was safe."

"I know you did."

"All I ask is that you stay in character until you're

out of the house. No sense giving it away too soon.''
He got to his feet, turned and extended a hand.

She took it and let him pull her up to her feet. ''Of
course I will.''

He walked around the bathroom, shutting off the
valves and faucets, then joined her again near the door,
slid his arm around her waist and spoke softly near her
ear. ''Stay close to me from here on. I don't want you
out of earshot until you're far away from danger.''

When he lifted his head away from her ear and
looked at her, she seemed to be searching his eyes, and
he thought her cheeks had warmed a little and wondered
why. But she only nodded, then stepped out of the bathroom.

Mel hugged Selene, not saying a word. Then she
hugged Kara and then Wes. She saved her mother for
last and hugged her hardest. Her mom whispered in her
ear that she would see her at the ranch soon, to keep
herself safe until then, that she loved her.

Mel hugged her even more tightly, nodding against
her mother's shoulder as if she agreed with every word,
even though she didn't. She couldn't. She'd been wrestling with this all morning, and she knew what she had
to do.

Wes would be driving the three women to Quinn in
a domestic-looking minivan that wouldn't raise a single
eyebrow. Just to be sure it didn't, ''Katerina'' and
''Thomas'' made themselves visible and vocal as the
van left. Anyone watching would know for sure they
were not sneaking along for the ride.

Alex put his arm around her, and they walked out
onto the front steps together, waving as the van
pulled away.

"So thoughtful of you to give the kitchen staff the afternoon off," she said in her soft Katerina voice, all for the benefit of the listening devices Alex assured her were nearby. "But then, you're always so thoughtful, Thomas. It's one of the things I love best about you."

"There was no in point keeping them here," he replied. "We have the ball tonight, after all." He hugged her a little closer to his side. "I hate being on display all the time as much as you do, you know, but at least at this event I'll have an excuse to hold you close the whole night through."

"As if you need an excuse," she teased, turning to smile up at him.

His eyes held hers, and her smile faded. Licking her lips, she leaned up closer, pressed her mouth against his. He sucked her lips gently, before letting them go free.

She didn't speak. She probably couldn't have, just then. And she didn't know why. It was just a kiss. Just a small, perfect, tender kiss. But it had felt…real. Natural. Not like playacting at all.

She turned away from him, hiding the reaction that one stupid little kiss was causing—not in her belly this time, but in her heart—and went back upstairs to the suite. When she had closed the door behind her, she stood there with her eyes closed tight for a moment, tasting him on her lips, wondering why she was going to do what she was going to do. Was it because of this ridiculous, hopeless crush she had developed on Alex Stone?

But she already knew it wasn't. At least not entirely. There were two other reasons. Two other very important reasons.

She went to the TV in the living-room area of the

suite, searching through the videos stacked on the stand beneath it. Choosing one, she dropped it into the player, closed the door, picked up the remote and thumbed the controls. Then she sank onto the sofa as the tape began to roll.

Katerina looked very much like her, Mel thought, wondering why she hadn't been able to see the resemblance before. But she was softer, more polished, more poised and *younger,* though not in age. Mel watched as the princess, looking every bit the part, walked down the aisle in a bridal gown that probably cost more, Mel thought, than every car she had ever owned, put together. The train dragged yards behind her. Thomas waited at the altar, for once without his sunglasses. His eyes were nothing like Alex's. His smile wasn't the same, either. It didn't make Mel's stomach clench the way Alex's did.

But he looked at Katerina with his heart in his eyes. And when she reached him and he took her hands in his, Mel found her own vision blurring.

She hit the pause button and sat there, looking at the couple. So young, so much in love. Kidnapped in some silly political game that would mean nothing in the long run. They might be facing death even now.

It wasn't fair. They had something so special between them. She'd seen it over and over, studied it. Secretly, she had envied it. It was wrong to let that special feeling be cut off. God, think how horrified tender little Katerina must be right now, to think of Alex—er—Thomas being shot. Executed. And Thomas—how helpless he must feel to be unable to protect his precious Katerina from that threat.

Katerina was so gentle. So timid and nonconfrontational.

Mel almost wished she could switch places with her. Let the kidnappers deal with someone who wouldn't flinch at fighting back, someone who would go down swinging and probably take out of a few of them with her.

But that was exactly what she was doing by being here and pretending to be Katerina. Fighting back. If Mel could keep the criminals uncertain about which of them was the real princess for just a little while longer, maybe Katerina could stay safe, and maybe her beloved could stay alive.

But if Mel left as planned, skipping out on the ball tonight—what then? Would the real Katerina live to see tomorrow's sunrise if she did? Or would the criminals assume that she had been whisked away to safety, and that the woman they held was the imposter?

She looked again at the pretty, delicate woman in white.

"I can't do it," she whispered. "It's not like the little wimp has a chance in hell on her own. I can't just throw her to the wolves to save myself. I can't."

Selene saw the relief in her mother's face, and in her sister's, too, as Wes drove them away from the mansion, the city and the need for pretense. Even after only two days, it was good to be able to speak freely and not watch every word. Different. Like having a gag removed.

Selene wasn't relaxed, though, and she could see very plainly that Wes wasn't, either. He glanced toward her, met her eyes, and silently acknowledged what she was thinking. This wasn't over. Mel was still in danger. Maybe more so than ever before.

Selene knew in her heart that she was going to have to go back there for her big sister.

It was a long, long drive from Austin to the small airport in the middle of nowhere. It would have been too easy to be traced from Austin-Bugstrom International. Wes had to be sure they hadn't been followed, so he took his time, drove over alternate routes, made unnecessary stops. The roads got narrower and bumpier the farther Wes drove. They stopped at a small-town roadside diner for lunch and a rest-room break. Only then did he seem to be satisfied that they were safe. He took them to the tiny airstrip, where a small plane was waiting, and a Secret Service agent took the van away.

By air it wasn't as bad. Kara and Vidalia napped, but not soundly enough that Selene could speak freely to Wes. She was dying to get him alone, to discuss what she sensed they both knew.

They landed at another middle-of-nowhere airstrip, got into another van and drove. It was nightfall by the time they passed the sign that said Welcome to Quinn, and Selene felt the most peculiar feeling steal over her like the soothing touch of a hot spring's water. When Wes turned onto the long dirt driveway and she saw the wooden arch that spanned it, with the words Texas Brand carved into it, that feeling grew. And when they drove underneath that arch, it grew even bigger.

The house was alight and alive against a backdrop of deepening blue sky. It reminded her of her own family home, that feeling of welcome that surrounded the place like an aura. Only, this house was far bigger, with a wide front porch full of rocking chairs and wicker furniture. The barn was three times the size of their own, obviously a working barn, not one used just for storage. It was huge and well kept up. Freshly painted, red with white trim. There were fences, and horses grazing, and, in the distance, dark shapes that might be cattle. But her gaze was drawn right back to that front porch again. There was a light on outside. And every piece of wicker furniture and every rocking chair, and even the steps, had people sitting on them. Men and women, children, babies.

"My, my," Vidalia said. "Just look at them all." She sounded a little sad.

"These are all…relatives?" Kara asked.

"Family," Wes told her. "There's a difference." He pulled the van to a stop and shut it off. "Not everyone is here. We thought it best for some reunions to take place in private."

Selene sent him a searching look. "What do you mean?"

He shook his head just slightly, exchanging a look with Vidalia. "It's not time yet. We'll wait for Mel. And there's plenty to deal with for right now. You ready?"

Selene nodded, but she thought her mother looked nervous.

Wes opened the door and got out. Then he went around the van and slid open the side door for Vidalia and Kara, helping them down, while Selene got out the passenger side. The four of them walked slowly toward the front porch as the Brands of Texas rose and stirred. Some waved; some smiled. A dark woman Selene recognized as Taylor, from Wes's photo of her, came running forward to greet him with a tender kiss. Then a man came forward, a very large man wearing a cowboy hat and a solemn expression.

He took his hat off when he got close to them. He

stopped walking, and stood there face-to-face with Vidalia Brand.

"Aunt Vi," he said. "I thought you were one of your daughters. You haven't changed at all."

She blinked at him. "You can't be Garrett?"

He nodded.

"What did they feed you, boy?"

He smiled at her. "Meat and potatoes, ma'am. It seemed to do the trick." But his smile died very slowly. "Aunt Vi…there have been bad feelings between our families in the past. I don't even know why, but—"

She held up a hand. "After my husband died, his brother, your father, tried to prevent me from keeping the Brand name. You see, John had another wife, another family. So his marriage to me was never legal. But I had five daughters by that man, Garrett, and they are Brands through and through. I earned the name, and I refused to give it up. Orrin disowned us. It's been that way ever since."

Garrett nodded. "I figured it was something like that. My father was a proud man, Aunt Vi. A stubborn man. And not always kind. But let me tell you something. My father and your husband are both gone now. I like to think they've made their peace on the other side somewhere. I think they'd like us to do the same."

Vidalia lowered her head. "I came, you know, after your mamma and daddy—the accident and all. I looked in on you. Of course they'd been gone two years before I even had word. But the second I did, I came." She shrugged. "I didn't know if I'd be welcome, though. And you seemed to be doing just fine on your own."

"You'd have been welcome. You're welcome now." He looked down at her, smiled broadly and opened his arms.

Vidalia went into them and hugged her big nephew hard. When he let her go, Selene saw tears in her mother's eyes and felt her own start to burn. She glanced at Kara, who had twin streams marking her cheeks.

"Come on, it's time you all get to know your family." Garrett slung an arm around Vidalia's shoulders and sent Selene a wink as the rest of the Brands came surging from the porch in one large, noisy mass.

It was going to be a long night, Selene thought. And a wonderful night, too. But even though she relished every hug, every welcoming face, every long-lost member of her family, she couldn't help but wonder just how long it would be before she could slip away, unnoticed, to make her way back to her sister in Austin.

And when she met Wes Brand's eyes across the crowd of relatives, she thought she saw the same thing in them.

Chapter 7

Alex tapped on the closed door of the master suite and waited a beat before opening it and walking in. "I thought you'd like to know—" he began, with his accent and his tux both firmly in place. But he stopped talking, stopped thinking—stopped *breathing,* really—when he saw Melusine. She looked…whoa. She looked good. The dress was strapless, black, shiny and tight. It hugged her all the way to her feet, except for the slit up the side. He liked the way her breasts swelled over the top of the thing. He liked that he could see the well of her navel beyond the clingy material. He wondered why the hell it had taken him as long as it had to see how incredibly sexy Mel Brand was. He'd pretty much come to terms with the fact that he liked her, that he was soft on her, that he was attracted to her. But how had he missed the fact that she was a knockout, a woman so beautiful that she could take a man's breath away, stop his heart and possibly cure cancer?

"Oh, stop it, already," she told him.

He blinked and forced his eyes upward from her cleavage to her face. "I'm— It's just— You look...*damn.*"

"Yeah? Well, you'd better take a picture, then, because I would rather wear a feed bag than this thing."

The illusion shattered. He lifted his eyebrows. "You don't *like* it?"

"Oh, it looked great on the hanger. But for crying out loud, Bernadette has me cinched up tighter than a rodeo bronc. I can't even draw a complete breath. And I don't know what to do with these things!" She glanced down at her breasts when she said it.

"I could, uh, maybe offer a few suggestions."

She shot him a glare. "Oh, very funny. This dress has them squashed up so high, I'm afraid they'll pop out at any moment."

"We can only hope," he whispered.

"What?"

"Er, nothing. I, um..." He cleared his throat, tugged at his suddenly too-tight collar and reminded himself of their roles. "Katerina, I know that you've always secretly detested formal wear, but surely, with all the functions we've attended together, you must be getting used to it by now."

"No."

"No?"

"*No.* No one could get used to this. Not in a hundred years. Will you *look* at these shoes?" She thrust her leg out the slit, so it was bare from midthigh down, save for the silk stocking and the stiletto-heeled, open-toed shoe.

"Lord have mercy," he muttered.

"What?"

"Have I ever mentioned that you have legs to die for?" he asked.

"I am practically standing on my toes."

He swallowed, his throat suddenly very dry. "Your buckle is coming undone."

"Well, it's not as if I can bend over to fix it in this sausage casing."

"I'll, uh…I'll get it." He bent down on one knee and slid his hands around her ankle, and the silk of her stocking brushed his fingers. He thought that he had never been so turned on in his life. My God, he was on fire. His hands were shaking like dry leaves in a brisk wind as he adjusted the strap of the shoe. His knuckles brushed her ankle. He cupped her calf in his palm, and for the life of him, he had to fight to keep from kissing her toes. What was wrong with him?

She lost her balance, had to bend forward, brace her hands on his shoulders. His hands shot to her hips to steady her. And then stayed there.

He rose very slowly, his hands still on her hips, hers still on his shoulders. Her face was very close to his. She smelled delicious, and he leaned a little closer.

She backed off almost imperceptibly, mere millimeters, but it was enough. He got the message. He thought about mentioning the chance of cameras, pretending this was just part of their act, but no. He wasn't going to make that mistake again. She was already angry enough about the last time he'd kissed her for that reason.

Or at least he thought that was what she'd been mad about.

"I'm going to be the envy of every man at that ball tonight," he told her softly.

He took a moment to brush a stray wisp of hair off

her forehead. She didn't look him in the eye, though. "Are you ready to go, then?"

"Yes. What was it you came in here to tell me?"

He lifted his brows, drawing a blank.

"When you first came in, you said you thought I would like to know…?"

"Oh, right. Our…friends…have arrived safely at their destination."

She nodded, getting the message. "That's a load off my mind."

"We'll have a new driver tonight. Our usual driver has the day off."

Again he saw that she understood. They would have to keep to their roles, even in the car tonight.

"Are you ready, then?"

"My, um, my wrap?" She nodded toward the back of the chair, where a black silk shawl with lace edging was draped.

He got it for her, came back, and draped it gently over her shoulders. He let his fingers skim the bare, warm flesh there, and he closed his eyes in secret hunger. God, what she was doing to him tonight.

He thought he felt her tremble when his fingers brushed her shoulder. But he couldn't be sure. Moving from behind her to stand beside her, holding her elbow, he walked her out of the room, into the hall.

At the top of the stairs she paused and turned to look up into his eyes. "I'm going to fall and break my freaking neck in these ridiculous shoes," she said.

It broke through the tension all this heat had created in him. Smiling, Alex slid one arm around her waist, bent at the knees and slid the other arm beneath her legs, scooping her up as he rose. "I can at least ensure that doesn't happen." He carried her down the stairs as she gaped at him.

"Al—er, Thomas, put me down. For heaven's sake, this is—"

At the bottom, he set her down again.

She drew a breath, smoothed her dress, then her hair. "I...thanks."

"Anytime."

She looked very confused as she searched his face. And no wonder. He was acting like a teenager with a crush. Hell. He took her arm again and led her outside to the waiting limo.

The ball was held at the governor's private residence, a mansion set on a sprawling ranch in the countryside. The Colorado River wound through the lush acre-wide backyard.

The ballroom at the mansion was utterly beyond belief. Mel couldn't get over the glittering chandeliers, the shiny marble tiles on the floor or the gems and diamonds glittering from the fingers, wrists and throats of all the women.

They were all so beautiful. So polished and charming. They knew how to laugh just so, how to flirt, how to dance. Oh, she could manage to move around the floor, but they were waltzing!

A string quartet played classical music in the front of the room. The place was packed, wall-to-wall bodies draped in rich fabrics and glittering jewels. People fluttered around her like mosquitoes in a swamp, and she started to feel claustrophobic as the governor's wife, hostess of this event, made introduction after introduction. She felt a complete fraud in her fake jewels and makeup, pretending to be someone she wasn't, someone she could never be.

Worst of all was the fact that Alex seemed to like her better tonight than he ever had before. When she was as little like her true self as she could possibly be.

It hurt. It shouldn't. But that didn't soothe the sting.

She clutched Alex's hand, even though she hated him right then, and he glanced down at her as if he adored every bone in her body. Even though she knew it was make-believe, that it wasn't her he was reacting to, she got warm and soft inside when he looked at her like that. He glanced at their hostess and the crowd milling around them, chattering. "If you'll excuse us, I've been waiting all day to dance with my wife."

"And who can blame you?" someone asked. It was a man, and his voice was dripping with meaning. "I hope I'll have the chance to do the same."

"I'm sure you'll have plenty of opportunities to dance with your wife, Mr. Monroe," Mel shot at him.

He blinked in surprise, but Alex tugged her away, onto the floor. Only then did she regret it, because as he swept her into his arms, she realized she was going to make a complete fool of herself if she tried to waltz. So she did the only thing she could do. She twisted her arms around his neck, pressed her body against his and rested her head on his shoulder. Alex's arms went around her waist immediately, and he bent his head to catch her whisper.

"I can't waltz," she told him.

"Thank God," he muttered.

Lifting her head, she blinked up at him.

"I hate waltzing. I hate the fox-trot, too. I hate all those things they taught us in prep school so we'd grow up to be socially acceptable young men."

She smiled slowly. ''I never would have guessed there was anything you didn't like about this posh, glittering world of yours.''

''Oh, there's a lot. Trust me. But for now, relax, we've got this part covered.''

''Do we? Don't you think anyone will wonder why we aren't dancing?''

''We are dancing. We're dancing like two people who would rather be at home making love.''

Her tummy twisted into a delicious little knot of longing when he said that. She thought she might have made a soft sound in her throat, as well, the way he looked at her.

''Which is exactly the kind of behavior that is expected of Thomas and Katerina Barde.'' His hand slid up the nape of her neck, fingers in her hair, and he pressed gently until she rested her head on his shoulder again.

His words made her shiver. But not as much as his touch did. It was a real effort to keep her head on straight with this man. Especially when his fingers skimmed some sensitive place that had never been sensitive before. The nape of her neck. The hollow beneath her chin, the small of her back. Or when his breath whispered close to her ear. It was a constant effort to remember that most of what he did and said to her was an act, part of the performance they were giving. And the rest of it, the flirting, the looks, those kisses—those things were directed at the woman she was pretending to be, not the woman she really was.

All things considered, she must be a complete idiot to be wishing she could drag him into the nearest coat closet and tear his clothes off with her teeth.

They danced. She pretended for just a little while that

it was she, Melusine Brand, he was holding so closely, so tenderly. She pretended that he meant it, even knowing that would only make it hurt more when she had to return to the reality where he didn't.

When the music ended, their bodies were pressed together as closely as if they had melted into each other. He was nuzzling her hair, she realized, and she was running her fingers repeatedly through his.

Without the rhythm to lull her, she woke from her warm fantasy, lifted her head, felt as if she needed to blink in the sudden light of reality. He smiled a little awkwardly and took her to a small table, grabbing two glasses of champagne and some tiny chocolate confections from a passing waiter on the way. She reached for a chocolate, but he grabbed it first and held it up to her lips.

''Don't you think this is overkill, Alex?'' she asked softly from beyond her false smile.

He shrugged. ''Too late now, everyone's looking.''

Angry with him, she took the chocolate from his fingers, drawing her lips over them in the process. Alex closed his eyes. She thought he shivered, and she also thought it served him right. She chased the chocolate with a large gulp of champagne, made a face and set the glass down. ''I would kill for a beer,'' she said, maybe to remind him of who she really was.

He smiled at that. ''I'll see if I can find you one later on.''

''Pardon me?'' a man said. It was the same man from earlier. Mr. Monroe. ''May I have this dance?''

''I...'' She shot Alex a look.

He smiled easily. ''I'm sorry, Monroe. But she is all mine tonight.''

Monroe reacted with surprise, but he nodded and backed off.

Alex got up and walked around the table, took her hand and drew her to her feet. "It'll blow our cover if you have to dance with someone else and they try to waltz. But the way you look tonight, the only way to keep them from asking is if I dance with you myself. All night."

"Oh...uh..."

He pulled her close, and they went on, shuffling very slowly around the floor with their bodies touching, hip to hip, thigh to thigh and head to shoulder, like teenagers at a high school prom. There was no way they could have been closer. At least not with their clothes on. It was heaven and hell, and she was aching for him and thinking maybe it wouldn't be so bad to indulge his fantasy for just one night.

She thought about that right up to the moment when the double doors at the far side of the room burst open and three men surged through them. A woman screamed, and a Secret Service agent yelled, "Gun!"

Alex reacted instinctively, pushing Mel to the floor, dropping to his knees, pulling his gun and covering her with his own body all at the same time, and all even before the first barrage of shots rang out.

"Crawl, baby. That way. Go!" He pushed her bodily, and she obeyed, crawling as fast as she could between the legs and feet of the now-panicked people who were running every which way. He pushed her underneath one of the tables that were draped with long cloths. Crouching, he held her tight to his chest, felt her shaking so hard he thought she would hurt herself while the shots rang out. Then the noise just stopped.

"I have to look," he whispered.

Nodding in jerky motions, she let go of him. He turned just a little, peered out between one tablecloth and the next.

"Alex, what's happening?"

He put a finger to his lips. One of the interlopers shouted for calm, for quiet, as the other two fanned out into the crowd, searching, he knew, for Thomas and Katerina.

Lowering the tablecloth, he crawled to the opposite side, lifted the cloth there, peered out. He saw French doors, four feet away. But if he opened them long enough to get out, the attackers would notice the open doors. Then he noticed the windows, with their long, velvet drapes. Most of the draperies were pulled open, but a few were closed. Fifty feet farther along the wall was the nearest one with closed drapes. There were tables lined up all the way there. He lowered the tablecloth.

The crowd was quieting now as the thug who appeared to be in charge told them that no one would get hurt, that they only wanted the little princess and her prince. And then they would go.

"Come on," Alex whispered.

"To where?" she asked. "Alex, I'm scared. Those bastards have machine guns."

He looked at her, saw that her eyes were damp and wide, and he knew it was a hellish thing for her to have to admit that she was afraid. He clamped a hand to the nape of her neck, pulled her face to his, pressed his forehead to hers. "Listen to me, baby, I know you can do this. You're not Katerina Barde, you're Melusine Brand. Now we're gonna crawl, quietly and carefully, but as quickly as we can manage, underneath these tables, all the way to the other end of the room. When we get there, we're gonna slip from beneath the table-cloth to behind the closed drapes at one of those big windows. Then we're gonna open the window, climb outside and get the hell out of here, and those bastards with the machine guns are never even going to know we left. Okay?''

''I don't know if I can do it.''

''*I* know you can do it. You're tough, Mel.''

''Damn straight, I'm tough. I meant, I don't know if I can do it in this getup.''

He glanced down at her feet, then reached for them, easing her shoes off. ''You have your gun?''

She nodded, hiking up her dress to reveal the little thirty-eight, tucked into a pancake holster buckled around her thigh like a garter. He heard a small voice telling him that this woman was like no woman he'd ever met in his life. He tried to ignore the other little voice telling him how much he liked that glimpse of her thigh. ''You go first,'' he told her. ''I want you in front of me.''

She got on all fours and began to crawl. The dress was too long, though, and her knees couldn't move far in it. After she stumbled for the third time, Mel stopped, sat back on her haunches and grabbed the dress at the top of the slit. Using both hands, she ripped, tearing several feet of length from the skirt. Alex grated his teeth, hoping to God the murmuring of the frightened people and the loud voice of the ringleader continuing to shout instructions as his men methodically searched through the crowd were enough to cover the sound of tearing fabric. Seconds later Mel was crawling again, in a drastically shortened skirt, with silky black panties underneath. He followed on his hands and knees, wondering just when he had become so unprofessional that he could think about a woman's derriere at a time like this. The way it moved, the nearness of it.

When she reached the end of the first table, she stopped. The tablecloth hung to the floor on the end of the table. The two legs were braced by a crosspiece that ran between them, about six inches up from the floor. Crawling up beside her, Alex lifted the tablecloth, only to see another, the one from the next table. He lifted that, as well. The tables were pushed together tightly. The movement of the cloths shouldn't be visible from outside. He held the cloths up as Mel carefully climbed over the crosspiece of one, then over the crosspiece of the next. She did it with painstaking care, knowing one wrong move could give them away by jarring the tables.

Once she was through, she held the cloths up for him to follow. And that was the way they continued, crawling, then maneuvering to the next table, until they'd journeyed the five table lengths.

"We should be just about there," Alex whispered. He lifted the section of tablecloth facing the rear wall and saw he'd judged right. The window was right there. It was very tall, with red velvet drapes hanging closed all the way to the floor. They would have to creep across about a yard of open floor to the draperies, and then the risk would be in causing the heavy fabric to move as they maneuvered themselves behind it. A distraction would be good.

"Ahh, what do we have here?" the leader asked.

Alex turned, peering out the other side of the table into the crowded room in time to see the man striding toward the row of tables on the opposite end of the room—the side where they had begun. Then Alex saw why. The scrap of black fabric Mel had discarded was lying on the floor, just peeking out from beneath the pristine white tablecloth.

Everyone was turning in that direction.

"Go. Now," Alex whispered.

The two of them scurried out from beneath the table to the window and behind the curtains. They knelt there between the drapes, the cool glass and the darkness outside, their hearts pounding, as Alex lifted his head to find the catch for the window. It was a handle in the center, four feet up, and the window would open outward. He reached up, opened the window, gripped Mel and jumped. It was five feet or so to the grassy ground, and they hit hard and rolled even as Alex was praying the thugs hadn't posted any guards outside.

Then he heard a man yell, "The window!"

Alex closed his hand on Mel's arm, drawing her to her feet and into a dead run. And somehow—God, he didn't know how, but somehow—they made it through the darkness to the river that backed the palatial home without anyone seeing them or shooting at them. But they were coming. He could hear them talking, searching.

They had to get the hell out of there, and fast. He scanned the riverbank. There was a small wooden dock, and a canoe bobbed serenely in the river, a rope holding it to the dock. He held her arm, ran out onto the dock. "Get in the canoe and lie down. Get your gun in your hand, you may need it. Be quick!"

He held the boat steady, and she obeyed without question. Except for the part about lying down. Instead, she watched his back, her gun at the ready, while he untied the rope and climbed in, rocking the little boat dangerously in the process. She holstered her gun and tossed him a paddle, then she turned around in her seat.

"I'm in the front, Alex. You're power, I'm direction, got it?"

"Yeah." He used his paddle to push off, then started paddling in earnest, going with the current. She was paddling, too, and within seconds they were surging down the river.

"We did it," she said, breathless, maybe even a little giddy. "We really did it, Alex. We got away."

He glanced behind them, saw forms gathering on the shore, looking after them. He hadn't seen any other boats, but that didn't mean there weren't any. "We're not in the clear yet, babe. Keep paddling."

"We'll be fine. They can't catch us. We can ride this baby all the way to—"

"They know where the river goes as well as we do, Mel. The faster we ditch this canoe and find another mode of transportation, the better."

She turned to stare at him, and she looked so profoundly disappointed that he wished he could take the words back. He expected her to argue. Instead she only nodded. "You're right. They have cars, if not boats. They're probably in them, racing downriver even now, hoping to intercept us." She glanced at the far shore, pointed. "Over there, you think?"

"As good a place as any."

They paddled hard for the far shore.

Chapter 8

It was 11:00 p.m., and it had been a long, long day. Selene had slipped away from the family as soon as she could manage it, even though she'd loved every minute she had spent with them all, to take a quick nap, but she couldn't sleep. Not even after all the others finally quieted and went to their own homes and their own beds. She crept down from the guest room she'd been sharing with Kara, tiptoed through the house and out the front door. Selene always went outside when she was troubled. Nature spoke to her, soothed her somehow, and always told her what she needed to know.

She sat on the Brands' wide front porch, rocking slowly in the swing. It was beautiful there. The stars winked from a huge sky over rolling meadows. She felt as if she were sitting in the middle of a painting.

She heard the screen door creak, turned her head and saw Wes Brand stepping out onto the porch. He had a mug in each hand and offered her one.

She took it, smelled hot cocoa and smiled. "How'd you know I was out here?"

He shrugged, taking a seat in the rocking chair next to the swing. "Lucky guess. I couldn't sleep a wink. You?"

She shook her head. "Not even a catnap."

"You feel it, too, then. Don't you? That something's happened?"

She nodded. "Yes. I do. I think they're in trouble. And I have to go back there."

"Mmm-hmm. I know you do. Me, too." He sipped his cocoa. "No one here is gonna like it."

"I wasn't planning to ask permission."

"I like the way you think."

She took a long drink, licked her lips. "This isn't a mix, is it?"

"There's a mix?"

Selene allowed herself a smile. "You know, you have a baby. A pretty wife, a family to take care of. You don't have to go with me."

"Course I do. You're family. I think it's best we get a good night's sleep and an early start tomorrow. That'll give us time to call your sister, check on things and book a flight."

She shrugged. "I was thinking I might just slip away, not tell anyone."

He shook his head. "You think no one would know where you'd gone?"

"Guess you're right." She shivered suddenly, wrapped her arms around herself. "God, something's really bad, Wes. Maybe we shouldn't wait for morning. Maybe we should go right now. If we drove all night…"

"Not yet."

She sighed. "I just wish I knew what was going on."

Inside the house, the jangling of a telephone shot through her like an electrical current. Wes didn't look surprised at all. In fact, he looked as if he'd been expecting it. He pressed his lips tight, got to his feet. "I think we're about to find out."

"Alex? Um, the water's moving faster." Mel didn't need to paddle anymore for speed, though she was trying like hell to paddle them toward the far shore. The little canoe was being swept along by the river at an ever-increasing pace. The water was dark and murky, and the tips of the little creases in the surface were starting to wear white frothy caps.

"I know. Just try to keep us from hitting anything and keep paddling."

"We're not going to make it."

"We'll make it. Keep paddling."

She was paddling as hard as she could toward the shore, but the current was getting faster and faster, and it was tugging them southward, not shoreward. A rock loomed, large and shiny wet.

"Damn." She thrust her paddle into the water on the same side as the rock, stroking fiercely, and, to her astonishment, she steered them around the boulder.

"Nice job!" Alex called.

It occurred to her that he'd had to raise his voice to be heard over the sound of the rushing water. Probably not a real good sign. And then another rock loomed, and she was too busy to think about anything else.

The nose of the canoe rose up and slammed down, water slapping them both in the face when it landed. It rocked and leaned. She worked by sheer instinct to keep the thing from flipping over and knew Alex was doing the same behind her. The far shore was no longer an option. The little boat was sucked into a vortex of foaming water and looming rocks, shooting and shuddering like a rocket in a meteor shower.

Her arms were too tired to keep fighting the water, and yet she kept on. The boat bounced so wildly she had to glance behind her once or twice just to be sure Alex hadn't been thrown out. He was still there, water dripping from his hair and face, his jaw rigid as he struggled to do his part.

Then, suddenly after what seemed like hours, the river eased up on them. She sat back, only then realizing she'd been kneeling in the bow to get more leverage on her paddle. "Thank God," she whispered. She was breathing fast, and her throat was dry, but every other part of her was soaked to the very skin.

His warm hand closed on her shoulder from behind. "Are you all right?"

"I'm exhausted."

"You're incredible. I've never seen anything like the way you—most women I know would have been cowering in the bottom."

"Then they'd have been in the river."

"I know, but—"

There was a sound. A loud roar. And they were moving faster again. "Oh, hell," she said, lifting her head and seeing what was coming. "Paddle, Alex. Paddle!"

He paddled, but the boat went over the waterfall, anyway. The nose of the canoe seemed suspended in the air for a split second; then it tipped downward, and Mel had to release her hold on the paddle to grip the sides or she would have flown straight out.

For a moment there was too much water in her eyes to see anything, and the canoe felt as if giants were beating it with hammers. Then there was some kind of impact, and her hands were jerked free of the wood she'd been gripping for dear life. And then she was in the water. Tumbling. She had no idea which way was up and which way was down. She couldn't breathe, and her body was pummeled by rocks and boulders. Every blow made her want to suck in a gasp of pain, but she clamped her jaw to prevent it. The last blow she felt was to her head. After that she didn't feel much of anything anymore.

Mel felt warm. That was the first thing that registered. Warmth. She'd been very, very cold, she seemed to recall. So the warmth was different. Surprising.

She smelled smoke. Not in a scary way, but in a nice way. Wood smoke.

She was being held. There were arms around her, a chest beneath her, for her pillow. Mmm, that was nice....

Oh, but her head hurt. The throbbing pain seemed to knock on her skull harder and harder until she noticed it above anything else. But only for a moment, because then she felt the rest of her body and realized everything ached. Pain was not nice....

But she was warm, and she was being held.

She didn't want to move. It was going to hurt to move. But she opened her eyes, mostly out of curiosity. She could see only blurry darkness at first. Then it was broken by the dancing yellow light of a fire and the gray clouds of smoke that billowed from it. The chest beneath her head was covered by a black suit jacket and was bare beneath that. The vee down the center where her cheek rested was just warm skin.

Alex, her brain told her.

She didn't want to lift her head, but she needed to see his face, so she tipped her head back as far as she could, in spite of the pain, lifting it only slightly. And she saw that chin of his and the whiskers he'd grown over the past three days and the line of his jaw. He was sitting on the ground, his back braced against a tree.

"Awake again?" he asked. He didn't move, except to lift his free hand and stroke her hair away from her face.

"Again?"

"You've been awake a few times since I pulled you out of the river. Just not very talkative or particularly coherent." He was looking intently into her eyes, even tugging her eyelids open a bit with his thumb.

"River?" Oh, God, yes. The canoe. The falls.

"How's your head?"

"It hurts. Everything else does, too. And I have a feeling that if I try to move too much it'll hurt more."

"Don't move, then." He gently pressed her head back to his chest. "We're not going anywhere for a while, anyway."

From where she lay, she could look around them, but only a little. What she saw wasn't encouraging. There were scraggly woods and wasteland. She saw a dilapidated building that might have been a barn once, its boards broken, warped and weathered to a pale shade of gray. Beyond that, there was only the night sky.

"Where are we?"

"Middle of nowhere, near as I can guess. I'd have taken you to a hospital if it were humanly possible, Mel. I carried you as far as I could, but there's just nothing out here."

"I don't need a hospital."

"You were shivering. I figured the best I could do was get you warm and dry."

"And I am warm and dry," she told him, snuggling against him, hugging her rough covers around her. Then she frowned and looked at the covers, touched them. "Is this...burlap?"

"I found some old feed bags in what's left of that barn over there. Sliced the seams, gave them a good shaking."

She blinked, slowly taking stock. Then she lifted the burlap to look underneath. "Am I wearing your shirt, Alex?"

"Your clothes were soaked." He sighed. "I didn't have a choice, Mel. I had to take them off you. I wrapped you up in the feed bags and hung our clothes by the fire to dry, but that dress was barely worth the effort. So when my shirt got dry, I put that on you instead."

"Oh."

"Are you okay with that?"

She relaxed against him. "Stop being such a gentleman, Alex. You didn't have a choice. How can I not be okay with that? You saved my freaking life."

He didn't say anything. She wished she could see his face and read his thoughts there. She wished she knew what he'd been thinking when he'd undressed her. She would give her eyeteeth to believe he'd entertained impure thoughts about her—*her,* not that trussed-up phony she'd been pretending to be. But she doubted it. The real Mel was not his type.

The silence stretched, tense and nerve-racking. "So how did you manage to build a fire?" she asked him at length.

"Took me an hour and a half. I was beginning to

think the Ranger Scouts were full of hot air, but that old rubbing two sticks together trick really works. After a while.''

"You were a Ranger Scout."

"Until I was nine."

"Why only till you were nine?"

"That's when I was packed off to military school. There was no Scout troop there. In a way the whole place was a Scout troop, though, so I didn't really miss it.''

"That's awful," she said softly.

"What is?"

"Being sent away to military school at nine. God, didn't you hate it? Weren't you homesick?"

He shrugged. "It was a great experience. Best thing my parents ever did for me."

She lifted her head, sitting upright this time. Her prediction had been right on the money: it hurt like hell. "Ow, dammit!" She pressed a hand to her head.

He did, too. "Easy. Lie still."

But she was too surprised not to look him in the face. "Are you saying you *liked* being sent away from home to military school at the age of nine?"

"Well, no. Not at the time. But now, with hindsight, I realize what a valuable experience it was."

"You're such a liar." She said it while rubbing her fingertips against her temples in small circles.

"I'm being perfectly honest."

"You're being perfectly correct. I'm not sure you know what honest is, Alex."

He frowned at her as if confused.

"Okay, let's say you get married. Let's say you have a son. When he's nine, would you pack him off to this same school?"

"No." He answered without hesitation.

"Why not?"

"Well, because...because..."

"It was a valuable experience, wasn't it? Best thing your parents ever did for you?"

"I didn't understand those things until later. Much later," he told her. "At the time it was..."

"What was it at the time?"

He lowered his eyes. "Awful. I hated it. Any kid that age would hate it. And I wouldn't put a child of mine through that. Are you happy now?"

"No, I'm not happy. My head hurts, and every part of my body aches, including a few parts I didn't know *could*. But I'm glad to see that you know the difference between good manners and honesty after all."

"And I'm glad to see you haven't suffered any brain damage. You're the same straight-up, in-your-face Mel you were before the blow to your head."

"You were hoping I'd wake up believing myself to be the real Katerina Barde, I'll bet."

He frowned so hard his brows touched. "Why would you think that?"

She rolled her eyes and looked away from him, getting to her feet, holding the feed bags around her shoulders. The ones on her lap fell away when she stood, though. She walked closer to the fire, saw the broken barn boards and deadfall he'd piled up nearby. There was a small stream off to the left. She heard it bubbling.

"Did you have some survival training at that military school?" she asked.

"Some," he said. "I think we should wait here until daylight. By then we might be able to get a better idea of where we are, so we can tell which direction is best to travel."

''We have to go west, don't we? Toward Quinn?''

''Quinn is hours away, even by car. What we need is a town, preferably one with a telephone.''

''Food and some clothes wouldn't be bad, either. And maybe some aspirin.'' As she said it, she rubbed her arm.

''You're covered in bruises,'' he said. ''I'm surprised you can even walk.''

She lifted her eyebrows but didn't comment. He'd looked her over pretty thoroughly, then, she thought. In the dark. By firelight, maybe. Should she be offended or flattered?

''I wish Selene was here,'' she said softly. ''She'd go forage in the woods over there and come back with enough herbs and roots and berries to make us a four-course meal with dessert, and probably brew me up some extra strength pain reliever in a tea while she was at it.''

He laughed a little. ''I take it you're hungry.''

''Starving.''

He sighed. ''We still have the guns. I could maybe…shoot something.''

She looked at him, smiling for the first time. ''Didn't they get wet?''

''I cleaned them, dried them. Used a bit of your burlap ball gown and a twig from a tree. Most of the bullets will be all right. Some might not fire, if any water seeped into the powder, but they're pretty well made these days.''

''If the bad guys are out looking for us, firing a gun might not be the best idea, though. Right?''

''Maybe not. Then again, they might be too far away. I think we traveled a good clip on the river.''

She tossed another piece of wood onto the fire, then

walked back to where he sat and returned to her spot close beside him. "I can wait for morning if you can." Then she leaned against him just as she had been before, placing her head on his chest.

Alex reached for the burlap sacks she had dropped and pulled them over her legs and his own. He slid them both to the side, away from the tree, so he could lie down, and she remained curled up tight beside him, embracing him.

He hoped to God there was a town nearby. A phone. Anything. Thank God she'd turned him down when he'd offered to shoot something for her dinner. Good grief, he didn't think he could remember how to field dress a game animal, especially without a knife. She would be shocked to learn he didn't carry a knife, wouldn't she? Didn't all rustic, manly men carry pocket knives capable of numerous tasks at all times? He would bet any one of her cowboy cousins would have had a side of venison roasting on the fire for her by the time she woke. And probably would have erected a shelter and made her a dress from the feed bags, to boot.

He had found it kind of cute to watch Melusine struggling to fit into his world. Kind of endearing. He'd liked that she needed his help, to tell the truth. With the manners and the dancing and the political correctness and the clothes and the makeup and the correct fork for the correct course. And maybe it had made him feel a little more important to be able to help her deal with all those things. Like the big hero, saving the helpless damsel.

But the wheel had taken a spin, and now it was his turn to feel inept and unequal to the task. It had been all he could do to get the damn fire going, and he'd cursed in frustration and thrown the sticks a dozen times before a tiny bit of hot-wood smell and a wisp of smoke had fed him enough encouragement to keep trying.

She wasn't used to men like him. He had thought he'd been impressing her with his social skills and ability to protect her back there in the world of the wealthy and powerful. But now, he realized, she was going to see him for the first time as the useless fop he was. Because out here, she was twice the man he was.

Wearing his white shirt, swathed in burlap, she snuggled so close to him that it would have been easy to believe…but, no. It was cold out here. She'd nearly drowned, been pounded mercilessly by the stones and the current. She was afraid, and he was the only person within reach. She was embracing him because of the situation and nothing more.

He lay there and he held her until the fire burned low and the sun began to rise.

Mel felt a coldness and a distinct sense that something important was missing. She opened her eyes to the sight of a blaze-orange sun peering over the distant horizon and what looked like miles of nothing stretching between her and it. Rolling acres of scrub brush and grass dotted by patches of gray-brown hardpack and hunching, odd-shaped boulders. Cactus. Tumbleweed. It wasn't desert in the sense most people thought of desert. It wasn't sand dunes and burning heat. But it was just as inhospitable.

And Alex was nowhere in sight.

That explained her sense of something missing. Alex. She got to her feet, letting the feed bags fall to the ground at first, then quickly snatching one up to drape around her shoulders in deference to the early-morning chill. The fire had died. Alex hadn't bothered to try to rekindle it. Where the hell was he?

"Alex?" she called.

There was no answer. He wouldn't have abandoned her here, she thought. Not deliberately. God, what if something had happened to him?

She quickly grabbed her little revolver from the flat rock near where she had slept. Alex had laid both the weapons there, within easy reach, last night. She scooped up the six precious bullets that still remained from where he'd laid them out to dry, then quickly poked them into the cylinder, gave it a spin, clapped it shut. The pancake holster lay near the charred remains of the fire, dry now, she hoped. She picked it up, felt it. Yes, perfectly dry. A little stiff. She worked the leather in her hands to loosen it up, then she strapped the holster around her thigh and slid the revolver home.

Yanking off her feed-bag shawl, the seams of which Alex had already ripped open, she wrapped it around her hips, knotting it at the right one. A nice sarong skirt, in burlap, with the open side providing easy access to her gun. Using her teeth she ripped strips off the remaining burlap sacks and wrapped those around her bare feet, which gave her at least some protection.

She was ready. She took a last glance at the fire to be sure it was out, and then she started walking, wondering where Alex would have gone, in what direction he would have started off before—before something had happened to him?

She looked around, wondering if he had fallen or been bitten by a snake, or if maybe those men with the automatic weapons had caught up with him. Was he wounded, hurt, bleeding? God, was he dead?

"Alex?"

There were hills and dips and trees and shrubs blocking her view, so she decided to get up higher for a better vantage point, scan the area for signs of Alex before taking off without a clue. The best spot, the highest spot with easy access, was a brush- and rock-strewn hill not far away, so she hiked in that direction and started up it. Not an easy task. Even with the burlap wrapping her feet, she kept slipping, so she had to grab hold of shrubs to help her pull herself along, and it was frustrating as all hell.

As she got near the top she heard movement and slowed down, creeping along, using cover, drawing her weapon.

Then she saw the man. His back was toward her, and he was standing underneath a large, gnarly apple tree that had seen better days. He was shirtless and lean, sinewy and tightly muscled. Smears of dirt and several scratches and bruises marred his back and shoulders. His hair was uncombed. He looked rugged. He looked dangerous.

"Turn around slow," Mel said, holding her gun at her side. She didn't point it at him. She didn't believe in pointing guns at anyone without cause, and she still wasn't certain she had one here.

He turned around slowly, frowning at her. "Morning, Mel. You sleep okay?"

She blinked twice before jamming her gun back into the holster, missing the first time and trying again. "I...didn't recognize you...without your shirt," she stammered. She had never really looked at him the way she was looking at him right now. Even though she'd been with him nonstop for days, she had never seen him undressed. She had never seen him like this, with his pants looking battered and his chest uncovered, his arms scratched and bruised and dirty, and his hair sticking up all over, his whiskers on the wild side.

This was not the immaculate gentleman in the designer suit. And it wasn't the imitation Thomas Barde. She didn't know who the hell this was.

O-hh, but she *liked* him.

"Are you all right?" he asked, searching her face, obviously confused by her reaction to him.

"Sure. Yeah, fine. I, um, I woke up and you were gone."

"I meant to be back before you woke. Sorry. I thought I could get a better look around from up here." He tossed something, and she jerked her hands up to catch it instinctively. "I found some apples."

"Thanks." She bit into one, puckered a little. Scrub apples, tart as hell. Mamma would say they'd make a great pie, she thought, but for eating off the tree they were sorely lacking. Still, her stomach was glad for the sustenance. "So what did you see from the top?" she asked between bites.

"There's a road off that way, and a few miles up, there's some kind of a building. It's too far to tell for sure, but it looks as if it might be a gas station."

"A gas station? Hey, maybe it would have soda and junk food. You know, I'll bet it would. And a bathroom with running water."

"And a phone," Alex said. "One highly unlikely to be tapped." He picked up his jacket from where it was hanging over a limb, pulled it on and started down the hill again.

She almost sighed in disappointment at him covering up his chest. He had a great chest. "Who will you call?" she asked, falling into step right behind him.

"Mick Flyte, back in Austin. He's got to be wondering about us by now."

"And you're sure you can trust him?"

"He's CIA. I know I can trust him."

"You ever hear the term 'oxymoron'?"

"You ever hear the term 'stereotype'? Mick's a good man. A good friend, but beyond that, he's the most dedicated person I've ever met. His goal is to get Thomas and Katerina back, safe and sound. He wouldn't do anything to jeopardize that."

"Okay, if you say so."

"I do."

He looked down at her, his eyes taking their time, skimming every part of her, taking note of the burlap skirt, the makeshift shoes. "How do you feel this morning?"

"Like I been 'ate by a wolf and crapped off a cliff.'"

He widened his eyes at her, flashing that killer smile of his. "That's got to be the most colorful answer I've ever heard."

She lowered her eyes and cussed herself. Why didn't she just scratch her backside and belch at him, while she was at it? Make a real impression?

Not that she wanted to make any kind of impression at all. In fact, she wanted him to see exactly who she really was.

And to want her anyway.

Man, she was pathetic.

Chapter 9

Had anyone asked Alex what sort of action hero he was most like, he would have probably chosen someone well mannered, well dressed, well-bred but effective. He doubted very much, though, that Melusine Brand would give a man like that a second glance.

Alex had no clever devices, no chewing gum explosives or cuff links that shot poisoned gas. So, all things considered, he decided the best way to deal with things from now on was to ask himself what John Wayne would do in a given situation and then proceed to do it. Mel couldn't very well realize how little confidence he had in his abilities to survive a trek through the desert if he acted like John Wayne, could she?

He'd seen the movies as a kid. How could he go wrong?

He was worried on several levels. He was worried about her injuries, things that might not show on the surface. He was worried about their lack of fresh water and the distance to the nearest speck of civilization. They couldn't go back toward the river without the risk of running into those machine-gun-toting thugs. He was worried about the enemies they were, inevitably, going to have to face down, just the two of them. And somehow, in spite of all the practical, logical worries on his mind, there was an impractical, illogical one shouting too loudly to be ignored.

He was worried that she would start comparing him to her cowboy cousins, and that she would find him lacking. He didn't want her thinking about how much better Wes or Garrett or any of the other Brands could handle themselves in the wilderness. How much better they could protect her.

In short, he wanted to impress the hell out of her with his raw, gritty toughness. The problem was, rawness and grit were not crops he'd spent much time cultivating.

No, the problem was that he was letting this kind of nonsense even enter his mind when they had practical things to worry about. Why did he care what the hell she thought of him, anyway?

He glanced down at her.

They'd been walking for two hours in silence. She was hurting, limping along in her rag-wrapped feet, and bone tired. It occurred to him that he knew exactly what John Wayne would do if he were the one walking along beside her.

Hell, why not? he thought.

He scooped her off her feet without so much as a word of warning, and he did it without even breaking his stride. She squeaked in alarm, lashed her arms around his neck and looked up at him as if he'd lost his mind.

"Uh, what do you think you're doing, Alex?"

"Carrying you."

"Yeah. I kind of picked up on that part. What I meant to ask is *why* are you carrying me?"

"Because you're injured and tired and sore, and I'm…"

"And you're what?"

"The guy. I'm the guy."

She stared at him with the funniest look on her face—the way she might look at a book she'd been reading if the words suddenly changed into some other language.

"You're the guy," she repeated.

He nodded.

"Well, you're going to be the *crippled* guy if you carry me that far. It's got to be another ten miles, at least. Put me down, Alex."

It *was* pretty ridiculous to think he could carry her all the way to the building he'd glimpsed. Now that the sun was up, it was getting damned hot. He stopped walking and set her on her feet, wondering just what in hell he was trying to prove.

She looked at him oddly, shook her head and started off again. "It was a really nice thought, though," she said.

He thought she sounded like she was tossing a bone to a mongrel dog, but…whatever. He trudged along beside her, not picking her up or offering to carry her again, and for the life of him, he couldn't guess what John Wayne might have done next.

They walked in silence, aside from the buzz of insects and the occasional cry of a hawk. It got hotter and hotter. It felt to Alex as if a flame thrower were aimed at them from above. It was more than two hours, probably closer to three, he thought, when they reached the road. Sticky bubbling tar stretched off into shimmering heat waves in either direction. They walked alongside it, not on it, because it was so much hotter than the baked, barren ground.

"You can carry me now, if you want," Mel said. She smiled just a little, but he could see the misery in her face. Her hair was wet, sticking to her sunburned cheeks and forehead. Her lips were already chapping.

He thought about telling her to carry him, instead. He felt as if he would surely sink straight to his knees if he tried. God, it was hot. But instead, he reached for her.

She slipped her hand into his, though. "I was kidding. Hell, you'd really do it, wouldn't you?"

"Try. Don't know how successful I'd be."

She shook her head and they walked on.

Finally they got closer to the weathered, brown, tinder-dry building that leaned slightly to one side. An ages-old gas pump sat in front. A fat man in overalls rocked in the shade, smoking a cigarette, a newspaper open on his lap. When he smiled at them, his face wrinkled like worn-out leather and was about the same color. Sun-browned to a shade of old copper.

"Well, now. You two get yourselves lost again, did ya?"

Alex frowned at him. Mel said, "You might say that. We had a little accident. Do you have a phone we could use?"

"Yep, in the back, don't you remember?"

"What do you mean, 'again'?" Alex asked.

Selene and Wes stepped into a limo from the private plane that had whisked them back to Houston. And for once Wes wasn't driving. The man in the back seat with them was one Wes had spoken to several times by phone but had never met face-to-face. He introduced himself as Mick Flyte, shook Selene's hand first, then Wes's.

"As I told you on the phone last night, Mr. Brand, there was an incident at the ball."

"Yeah, and that's all you told me."

"No," Selene corrected. "He told you they were still alive. That's important."

The man's gaze shifted just slightly, downward and to the left.

"Maybe it's time you elaborated a bit on this 'incident,'" Wes suggested.

Flyte nodded. "Gunmen stormed the ball in search of Katerina and Thomas. Alex is quick on his feet, though. He managed to get himself and Miss Brand out through a window, and they had a fairly decent head start before the gunmen realized they had left the party."

"And then?" Wes prodded.

"There was water," Selene said. "I know they were in the water. I knew it last night."

Flyte blinked at her, his brows going up. "How could you know that?" She only shook her head, so he went on. "There was a canoe missing from the dock. We surmised Alex and Miss Brand took it and headed southward on the Colorado River."

He stopped there, again averting his eyes.

"Please, just spill it, Flyte. There's no point in dragging this out. We need to know, and we need to know it all if we're going to be any help to you."

Sighing, Flyte nodded. "That stretch of the river gets pretty rough. Rapids, some falls. It wouldn't have been an easy ride, even for an experienced person. We're worried they may have lost it, wound up in the river themselves.''

"I think that's exactly what happened," Selene said softly. "I know they were in the water. I felt it, I felt the cold and the wetness, and terrible pounding. Rocks, I think.''

His brows pressing against each other, Mick Flyte glanced at Wes.

"She's something of a psychic. Especially where her sisters are concerned.''

"Really. That could be very helpful in this.''

Selene narrowed her eyes on the man. "Don't you dare patronize me, Mr. Flyte. I know things, and I really don't care whether you believe it or not.''

"I wasn't patronizing you, Ms. Brand. We have several people like you working for us in various agencies within the government. While we don't advertise it to the general public, we are fully aware that there is a great deal more to psychic ability than formerly believed.''

She stared at him for a full minute as the car rolled onward, still unsure, Wes thought, if the man were serious or somehow teasing her.

Then he asked, "Do you get the feeling they're still alive?''

"I don't know. I get extremes, you know? When she was in the water, I felt the cold, the pain of the rocks. Then there was nothing. I don't think I'll get anything until she's feeling another extreme.''

He nodded. "Let me know if you get anything. We can use any—" He broke off as his cell phone beeped, and he yanked it from his pocket to answer it. Speaking briefly, he glanced at Selene, then Wes, and tucked it back into his pocket. He pressed the intercom button and spoke to the driver. "Take us south, I'll tell you where to turn off."

"Yes, sir."

"What is it? What was that call?" Wes asked.

Sighing, Flyte said, "They found the canoe. Or…what was left of it."

The old man shrugged, getting to his feet as if it were an effort. He opened the rickety door and held it for Mel, who hurried inside, blinking in the dimness and scanning the place for a telephone.

Alex scanned it, too. The place was packed with inventory. Canned foods and cold drinks, a rack of sunglasses, even some clothes. Everything looked and smelled brand-new. Mel seemed to forget about the phone when she saw the merchandise. She went to the cooler first, grabbing a bottle of water, twisting off the cap and taking a long drink.

Alex watched her throat move as she swallowed. When her head came down again, she passed the bottle to him, turned and went to the clothing rack and started flipping through the blue jeans that hung from wire hangers.

"I guess you'd better start a tally," he told the old fellow. Then he finished the bottle of water.

Mel took a pair of jeans, snagged herself a white T-shirt with an American flag on the front and dropped to her knees to examine the row of suede hiking shoes.

"Phone's in there," the old man said with a nod toward the back. "But if you're gonna call them folks who picked you up the last time, you'd best tell 'em to bring some cash along. They left without paying for your meal last time."

"Last time?"

"Sure. Oh, don't tell me you don't remember...." The old man squinted and looked more closely at Alex. "Maybe you *don't* remember. You ain't him. But *she's* definitely *her*. I wouldn't forget a face that pretty."

Mel was already vanishing into the door marked Rest Room with the clothing and a bottle of sunburn remedy.

"You're telling me she's been in here before?" Alex asked. "With a man who looked something like me?"

"Just two days ago," the old man said.

"And someone came and picked them up?"

"Yep. I was in the back, getting some more eats for 'em, and when I came out, they were leaving. There were two of them SUVs out front, and four or five men hustling 'em into the back of one. They took out of here spewing dust for a hundred yards and never even paid for their meal."

"In what direction?" Alex asked.

The old man pointed.

Nodding slowly, Alex patted the old man's arm. "Now, this is very important. Is there any place within walking distance that couple could have come from?"

The old man shrugged. "I figured their car broke down."

"But what if it didn't? What if they were holed up somewhere nearby? Where would the most likely place be?"

"There ain't but one place, mister. Though I don't know why you couldn't just ask your lady friend. It's fifteen miles into the desert, due west. Used to be a military base out there, but it's been abandoned for years. It's the only thing around for fifty miles."

Mel stepped out of the rest room. "God, that's so much better than burlap," she said. Her hair was wet and smoothed back. She must have washed up back there. She wore jeans, a T-shirt, a pair of small-size men's hiking boots and a khaki button-down shirt.

"So did you call someone?"

"Not yet."

"Why not?"

"Because Jake here has been telling me that you've been here before and left without paying your tab, with four or five men in SUVs."

She blinked, looking at him, then the old man.

"The name's Sonny," he said.

"You think it was…?" Mel asked softly, searching Alex's face.

"Could be. Look, there's an abandoned military base fifteen miles into the desert. If we could get to it, check it out…"

"We could save them."

"Save who?" Sonny asked. "You tellin' me you ain't that pretty girl was here before?"

"No."

"And she's in some kinda trouble?"

"Yes," Mel said. "And if you tell anyone we've been here, we'll be in trouble, too. Can we trust you to keep quiet?"

"You bet."

Alex met Mel's eyes and nodded. "I'll call Mick Flyte. You'll stay here where it's safe and wait for help to arrive. Meanwhile, I'll hike out to this base and try to keep an eye on things until we have more help."

She crossed her arms over her chest and tipped her head to one side. "Right. As if you have a chance in hell of going out there without me."

"I'm perfectly capable of hiking through the desert."

"So am I. What I'm *in*capable of is sitting on my hands while someone I care about risks his life."

"Look there's no sense in both of us risking... Someone you care about?"

She just shrugged and turned to the old man. "We're gonna need some backpacks. Water. A couple of blankets and some matches in case we get stuck out there overnight. And food. God, I'm starving to death."

"And bullets," Alex said. "I don't suppose you carry any ammo?"

"This is Texas, son. Everybody carries ammo." He handed Alex a pad of paper and a pen. "Take what you need, get those packs put together and keep a tally. I'll fix you some sandwiches to eat before you go."

Alex placed the call, and the sense of relief that washed through him when he heard his friend's voice on the other end nearly floored him.

"Alex? Thank God. Where the hell are you? What's going on?"

"Is the line secure?" Alex asked.

"It's my personal cell phone. Yes, Alex, it's fine. Go ahead."

"Look, we escaped the attack at the ball, took a wild ride down the Colorado—hell, I don't know how far. We went over some falls, and the canoe got smashed to bits."

"We found the wreckage. Are you and the girl all right, Alex?"

"She took a hell of a beating. She seems to be all right. I can't be sure...."

He heard Mick speaking to someone else. "They're all right." Then, to Alex again, "Tell me where you are. We'll come and get you."

"Who's with you, Mick?"

"Two of the Brands. Wes, and the younger sister, Selene."

"Keep them out of this," Alex said.

"I'm not sure that's going to be possible, but I'll do my best. Now tell me what happened."

"We hiked out of the desert—west, going by the position of the sun—maybe a dozen miles until we came to a road. Found a small general store here." He turned toward the old man. "Where are we, Jake?"

"Closest town is Rock Island," he said. "The road out front is 155."

Alex repeated the words.

"We'll find it."

"Wait, Mick, there's more. The owner, he said a couple who looked like us had been here before. Said the woman and the man she was with left without paying for their food, that they were hustled away by several men in SUVs. I think our couple may have managed to slip away from their captors and get this far, only to be retaken."

Mick swore softly.

"The storekeep here, Sonny, says the only habitable place within fifty miles is an abandoned military base fifteen miles west, into the desert. We're loading up on supplies and hiking out there."

"No, Alex. You should wait for us."

Alex shook his head even though he knew Mick couldn't see him. "You need to put this together just right, Mick. Men on the ground, as quiet as possible. You can't come in with choppers and Jeeps, or they're liable to slip away again, or, worse yet, panic and kill the hostages. Take your time, do this right. We will head out there to keep an eye on things, assess the situation and try to keep our two lovebirds alive until you and the guys can get out here."

"Are you sure about this?" Mick asked.

"Yeah. We've come this far. We'll be fine."

"All right. Be careful, Alex."

He'd watched Mel work methodically the entire time he'd been on the phone with Mick. She'd gathered supplies and kept track of them all on the old man's notepad. Then she laid everything out on a large table and proceeded to pack it into two matching backpacks. Just as Alex was hanging up the phone, she handed him a pair of jeans and a T-shirt like hers, along with a khaki button down much larger than the one she wore.

"Are we going as twins?"

"You can't hike in dress pants, and those shoes are a joke. What size are your feet?"

"Eleven," he told her, taking the jeans and shirts. She nodded, walked to the row of shoes and grabbed him a pair.

"Go on into the rest room and wash some of the dust off," she advised. "I felt loads better after I did."

He nodded. "I don't suppose there are showers?"

"No, just a sink and lukewarm running water with complimentary rust. But it's wet."

"Wet sounds like heaven about now."

She was right, he thought as he stripped down in the rest room and washed up as best he could. He wasn't exactly dressed for rough-and-tumble work. And it did feel great to rinse away a few layers of desert. He made it quick, ever mindful of the two people whose lives were in the balance out there somewhere.

When he emerged again, Mel was at the small wooden table munching a sandwich and drinking more water. A small plate across from her held another meal. Behind the counter, Sonny was scribbling on the notepad, totaling up the damage. He looked at Alex with a toothy smile. "That'll be $209.75, with the tax," he said.

"Pay the man and eat. We need to get going," Mel told him. "I'm sure he takes plastic."

"Oh, yeah. I can do that."

Alex pulled his billfold from the jeans he now wore, and reached for his titanium card, then thought better of it and counted out cash. The bills had been soaked, dried in the wallet and were kind of stuck together, but they would have to do. Then he sat down opposite Mel and ate.

He was nervous as hell. Not about going up against international criminals. He'd faced down dangerous men before, and he had no qualms about doing it again. It was all this outdoorsy stuff that was bothering him. He supposed he'd handled it as well as anyone could have, so far. But hell, he was out of his element, and he knew it. If he'd been left to choose the supplies and pack the backpacks, he would have been guessing, at best. Mel seemed to know exactly what to bring and how much of it.

And despite the fact that she had to be hurting, tired and frightened, she was glowing right now. Her eyes sparkled with energy.

She was finished with her sandwich already, so she got to her feet and came to where he sat. Taking a plastic container of sunblock from the table, she squeezed some into her palm, rubbed her hands together a few times and then pressed them to his forearm.

Alex went dead still, stopped eating his sandwich and just sat there, looking at her hands on his skin. She didn't seem to notice that, though. She worked the lotion over every exposed bit of flesh on his right arm, all the way to his hand. When she smoothed the lotion over and between each finger, he wondered why it felt to him like the world's most erotic foreplay, then kicked himself for being an idiot.

He flexed when she began again with the second coat. He couldn't help it, wasn't even sure it was premeditated, but he did it, and he felt her hands slow as they moved over his biceps, felt them linger there. He stole a glance at her eyes just as she closed them, swallowed hard and moved her hands away.

She repeated the entire process with the other arm, then pulled her chair closer and squeezed more lotion onto her hand. "Put your head up."

He lifted his chin. Her hands moved to his neck, warm and efficient. The lotion smelled like coconuts and vanilla beans and hot sandy beaches and summer sunlight. Her palms slid over his nape, and he shivered.

"You're already starting to burn. So was I. It'll be sore as hell when we have time to sit still and feel it."

She ran her hands over his pulse points and underneath the edges of his collar, and everywhere she touched, he felt the dull pain of a slight sunburn and the raging fire of wanting her.

"Close your eyes," she said.

Was her voice a little softer? A little coarse? No, it was probably just the long walk in the desert this morning. He closed his eyes. Her fingertips danced over his forehead and nose, his cheeks, the parts without three days' growth covering them. He suddenly wished he had time to shave.

"Sonny drew us a rough map," she said softly. "We've got fifteen miles of desert to cross. I got us a compass, so we shouldn't get lost. If we do, we're history."

"We won't get lost," he promised.

She nodded, took a pair of sunglasses from the table and slipped them on his face. Then she plunked a Western hat on his head. It was made of straw, cool, with a wide, shade-giving brim. ''We need all the protection from the sun we can get.''

She put her own sunglasses and matching hat on her head. ''Ready for the backpack?'' she asked him.

He nodded, stood up and turned around.

Mel hefted his backpack, and slid it over his arms and shoulders as he hunched it into place. ''Great,'' she said. ''Now you do me.''

He spun around and reached for the sunblock so fast he knocked the bottle over. Mel said, ''No, not that. I already smeared enough of that on to cover three people.'' She snapped the cap closed and dropped the bottle into the remaining backpack, then turned her back to him. ''I meant the pack.''

He lifted the pack from the table. Then he shook his head. ''No way in hell, honey. Uh-uh. You aren't carrying this much weight.'' He set the bag back down, took his own off, as well, and went to work. He removed the huge water canteen from the side of Mel's pack and attached it to his own. He took the box of ammo from hers and added it to his. Then he took the sleeping bag off the bottom.

''Oh, come on, we're gonna need that!''

''There's one in my pack,'' he said, patting the neatly rolled bundle.

''Well, yeah, but—''

''That'll be plenty.'' He lifted her pack again. ''It's still heavy.''

''I'm still perfectly capable of carrying it,'' she told him and, turning, thrust her arms through the straps and hefted the weight easily.

Alex frowned.

"What did your friend Mr. Flyte say?" she asked as she helped him back on with his own pack. Together, they walked out of the building, into the burning heat.

"They're going to try to get some satellite photos of the base before they do anything. They don't want to waste manpower on a whim. If there's any sign of Katerina and Thomas, they'll send in special forces, nice and quiet, totally unannounced. It'll take some time, but it's better than charging in like bulls and spooking them." He sighed. "Chances are they've moved on by now, anyway."

"Why the hell would they? They've got the perfect hideout. In the middle of nowhere."

"Yes, but the couple were seen. They may not have risked staying around here after that. Certainly once they get what they want, they'll have no reason to stay."

"What they want is Katerina and Thomas dead." She said it, then she blinked and stared at him. "God, do you think...?"

"No. I don't, and you shouldn't, either. You start thinking that way, you won't have the heart to get through this. Besides, that's not what they want, not really. They want Tantilla. They want enough leverage to use to force President Belisle to give it to them."

She nodded her agreement. "Once they know they have the real Katerina, then they have that. Do you think they'll try to take her out of the country?"

"I don't know. I guess we'll find out when we get out there."

She nodded her agreement. "Let's go."

They crossed the dusty, barren road, popping tar bubbles with the clean soles of their new shoes, then striding onward, leaving the road and the little shop far, far behind them.

Chapter 10

It was hot and growing hotter, Alex thought, with every step they took. Walking wasn't easy, as the hardpacked, barren earth softened and changed into the shifting sands of pure desert. The farther they hiked, the hotter it grew. There had been trees, scrubby and bare, brush, back there near the road. Here there was nothing except cactus and the occasional boulder. Red rock formations standing tall and oddly shaped in the distance.

"They picked a hell of a spot to put a military base, didn't they?" Mel asked.

He'd been watching her closely, unable to comprehend how she could manage to look strong, confident. He was damp with sweat within the first hour and could see that she was, as well. They had walked maybe five miles, and he decided it was time for a rest.

"Come on, let's take a break. Over here." He took her arm and led her toward the minuscule shade offered by a boulder. They took off their packs, sat down and leaned back against the warm rock.

Alex freed a canteen from his pack, twisted off the cap and handed it to Mel. His own mouth felt about as parched as the ground they'd been walking over, but he figured both John Wayne and James Bond would see to the lady first, so he could do no less.

She drank in small sips, swishing each one around her mouth before swallowing. Then she poured a bit of cool water into her cupped palm and patted it on her face and the back of her neck.

"The water's already warm," she said, handing the canteen back to him. Their fingers brushed, and hers were moist and hot.

He drank from the canteen. The lukewarm water tasted unreasonably good to his parched mouth.

"I don't know when I've enjoyed water so much, do you?" she asked as Alex put the cap back on, making sure it was good and tight, before reaffixing the canteen to his backpack and leaning back against the boulder again.

"I was just thinking that," he said. "Though I have to say, an ice-cold beer would hit the spot a little bit better right about now."

"Ice-cold beer, huh?" she asked.

He nodded. "Why that doubtful expression?"

She shrugged. "I just took you more for a fine wine kind of guy," Mel said, smiling at him.

"What, you don't think a 'fine wine kind of guy' can enjoy a cold beer every now and then? There's more to me than you give me credit for, Mel. I'm multilayered."

She lifted her brows and studied him. "Are you trying to tell me that there's a redneck hiding underneath that *GQ* model exterior?"

"Just as much as there's a little bit of princess hiding behind your rough-and-tumble cowgirl surface."

"That wouldn't be much." She shook her head, closed her eyes behind the sunglasses she wore and let her head rest back against the boulder. They were sitting as close as they could without touching. "I've gotta tell you, Alex, that role I was playing was a terrible strain. As much as I hate to admit it to a man like you, I don't enjoy embracing my inner princess the way most women would. The hair and makeup and manners. The damn shoes alone…" She shook her head slowly. "I don't suppose that comes as any surprise to you, though."

"No. Just makes me curious."

"About…?"

"About why it is that you hate to admit that to a man like me." He was facing her, trying to read her expression, but it was tough behind the sunglasses. And she wasn't looking at him, either. He thought maybe her eyes were closed behind the shades. She must be exhausted.

She shrugged her shoulders just slightly. "Because you like all that stuff in a woman. And you liked it in me, I know you did. But it was all just as phony as…as the desert backdrop in a cheap western."

He blinked at her.

"You know, those old cheesy films, where all the Indians were played by Caucasians?"

He nodded. "I know the kind you mean."

She shook her head a little. "I guess this whole adventure reminded me of those. They were so tacky, but I loved them anyway. Especially when the cowboy pulls a guitar out of his saddlebag and starts singing."

Alex sang the opening notes of one such cowboy

song, drawing out the words, "Bluuuuuuuuuue…shadooooow…" A smile split his face when she joined in with the next line. Neither of them could remember what came next, and they both stammered to a halt and started laughing.

The laughter died slow. He reached up to her, plucked the sunglasses off her face. "You want to know what I like in a woman, Mel? I like that she's watched campy old westerns so often she knows some of the words to that song."

She blinked in surprise. "Really?"

"Yep." He put her glasses back on. Not because he was through wanting to plumb the depths of her eyes, but because she was squinting in the setting sun.

"I'm surprised. I mean, I wouldn't have guessed that you would like that kind of film."

"What, goofy comedy? It's my favorite genre."

"Mine, too," she said.

He smiled. "They're crude, rude and completely inappropriate. But they're funny as hell."

She laughed softly. "My mother refuses to let me watch the worst of them while she's in earshot," Mel said, shaking her head.

"You can always come watch them at my house."

He turned toward her when he said it, found his gaze stuck to her lips like a fly on flypaper. He licked his own, wished they weren't so dry, leaned in closer and brushed hers with them.

For just a second he felt her soften and respond. But then she turned her head away. "I…we should get moving."

"Yeah. All right." He got to his feet, reached down a hand to her.

She took it and let him help her to her feet. "How far do you figure we've come?"

"Five miles, maybe. We won't make as good time from here on in, given the terrain."

"And the heat," she said. "So, ten miles to go. Another two hours of this."

"More like three."

She shook her head as they trudged along. "You know, if Katerina and Thomas got away and made it all the way to that store…" She stopped there, shaking her head. "It's tough for me to believe Katerina ever made it that far."

"Why? I mean, you're not having any trouble so far, are you?"

"No, but that's me. I'm not Katerina. I'm used to hard work, and I'm pretty strong. But for the woman I was pretending to be for the past few days, with her coddled lifestyle and her ridiculous shoes, to hike fifteen miles through the blazing hot desert? I just don't see it."

He sighed, frowning as he thought it through. "What seems off to me isn't that they made it fifteen miles, it's that their captors didn't catch up with them before they got all that way. I mean, for crying out loud, it was two people on foot versus four or five men, probably armed, in four-wheel-drive vehicles."

"Maybe they sneaked out in the middle of the night and no one noticed they were gone until morning."

"I suppose that's possible," Alex said.

"Yeah, that's probably it." They walked a few more steps, and Mel spoke again. "I don't know, though. How would they have known which way to go?" She shook her head, glancing down at the compass she'd been checking periodically, then left and right, ahead and behind. "I mean, everything looks the same out here. Without the sun and this compass, I wouldn't know which way we were going."

"Maybe they used the stars?" Alex suggested.

"Yeah, they seem like real outdoor-types. Probably know all about using the stars to guide their way."

"You're right. It's not likely," Alex said.

"And what about my earlier observation? That this was one odd place to set a military base?"

"Well that, at least, makes some kind of sense. If it were a secret base, which it must have been, since Mick and I never heard of it, then it would have to be set up in some remote area."

"Like Area Fifty-One?" she asked.

"Without the aliens."

"We can only hope," she said.

At the riverbank Mick Flyte stood beside the limo, with a map spread out on its hood. Wes stood beside him, leaning over and peering at it. "Alex said he was calling from a gas station and general store of some kind. But I'm damned if I can see one on this map."

Wes studied the map, which was unlike any he'd ever seen. It had every detail listed, every business marked. But there was no store like the one Alex had described.

And according to Flyte, there was no military base out here, either.

"Can we even be sure it was Alex on the phone?" Wes asked. "I mean, could it have been an imposter? An attempt to divert our attention from where we need to be looking for them?"

"I thought of that, too," Flyte said. "Damned if I could swear to it—the connection wasn't the greatest, but I think it was Alex's voice."

"Maybe it was. He could have been forced to make the call," Wes said.

Flyte shook his head slowly. "I doubt anyone would have much luck forcing Alex to do anything he didn't want to do. He can take more punishment than anyone I've ever trained. I tried like hell to get him to come to the CIA with me, but he wanted no part of it. No, they could torture Alex till hell froze over, and it wouldn't do them any good."

Wes said, "They wouldn't need to torture him at all. All they'd need to do is threaten to hurt Mel."

Flyte met Wes's eyes, and Wes could see the man knew he was right.

Several Jeep-loads of military types pulled to a stop along the riverbank, spilled out and began to organize into groups. There were other groups starting to search from other points, about thirty miles in every direction. Flyte wanted to start from the site of the wrecked canoe, since the location Alex had given by phone had been no help at all, and he insisted Wes and Selene come with him. Wes suspected the man was hoping Selene might be able to pick up on something there.

It had taken two hours from the time of Alex's call to get things organized to this point, and Wes was just about jumping out of his skin with impatience.

Selene, though, didn't seem to be paying much attention to the amount of time that was ticking by or to the groups of armed men in tan-colored camo. She was too busy staring at what remained of the canoe.

It had hit Wes pretty hard, too, when he'd first seen it. It had been battered to bits against the rocks, and he couldn't help but wonder how her sister's body could have withstood the same treatment. He figured she was probably wondering the same thing about now.

Flyte took his map and went to join the soldiers who had arrived, so Wes walked over to Selene, stood beside her.

"I just keep seeing it, feeling it in my mind," she said softly. "Mel being lifted by the water, then smashed down against the rocks, lifted and smashed, over and over. Plunged beneath the waves and held down, pummeled some more, her lungs starving until she finally broke the surface and..." She gasped out loud, clutching her chest and sucking in all the air she could hold.

Wes grabbed her shoulders in a firm grip. "Easy, take it easy."

Flyte looked up from where he was, spoke quickly to the men and hurried to join Wes and Selene at the water's edge.

Straightening, Selene stared hard at Wes, though he got the feeling she wasn't really seeing him. She said, "She's alive. It's hot. God, it's so hot, and she's tired. And she's hurting. Her head. Her back. One foot is sore. There's this weight...on her back, and her throat is dry and..." Selene wiped imaginary sweat from her forehead. "She's with Alex. Yes." Then finally she focused. The distant look left her eyes, and she looked from Wes to Flyte and back again. "I think the call was legitimate," she said finally. "I think my sister is walking through the desert right now with Alex."

"Well, there's no military base and there's no store on the map, so there's no way for us to tell where to begin looking for them," Flyte said.

"There's got to be a mistake," Wes said. "Look, Flyte, you said yourself how good Alex was, how sharp. If he said he was calling from a store, then he was. Maybe it's not on the map, but it's there. It has to be.

We find that little store they made that call from, and we go due west, just as Alex said he was going to do.''

"The store had to be within walking distance from here,'' Selene said, nodding. "Is there *anything* on the map? Anything at all? A town, or even a crossroads?''

Flyte shook his head. "No town. But there are only a couple of paved roads within any reasonable distance. Not the one he gave on the phone. That's fifty miles south. Still, let's check them out, drive over them, see if we can find this store that didn't make the map. I can't think of a better idea than that right now. Can you?''

Wes shook his head, and Selene did, as well.

"Then that's the plan,'' Flyte said. "I'll have the troops head into the desert to search for signs of them while we look for the store.''

Mel wasn't walking so much as dragging her feet along the ground, weight on the left, pull the right, get it underneath, shift the weight, drag the left. Her legs were heavy, leaden, and one foot was still sore from the blisters she'd developed while wearing feedsack wrappings for shoes. Her entire body was wet. Every time she stopped for a drink of water, she felt she was only refilling her sweat ducts so they could keep soaking her. Her head pounded mercilessly, and it was maddening to keep fighting the urge to pull off her clothes in deference to the heat. She kept telling herself it would be hotter without them, but her body didn't really believe that. She'd given up reapplying sunblock hours ago. It swam off her skin as fast as she rubbed it on. Besides, she didn't want to move anything more than was absolutely necessary.

"Here. Over here,'' Alex said. His voice was odd,

kind of hoarse as if he had a bad cold. He took her arm gently, urging her to the left, where a giant prickly cactus created a pool of shade on the parched ground. The shady spot was small. Alex made her sit down there, then took a spot beside her, but he wasn't shaded at all. He took her backpack off for her, then his own, and then he brought out the canteens, handing one to her and tipping the other to his own mouth.

She took off her sunglasses and bathed her nose in cool water. The shades kept sliding down, because of the sweat, and she kept pushing them back up until the friction had worn sore places on either side of her nose. It hurt. Everything hurt.

"I don't understand, Alex. We've been walking due west for hours. We have to have come fifteen miles by now."

He twisted his wrist to look at his watch, then remembered he'd taken it off. She knew why. It had gotten too hot for him to bear having the metal touching his skin. Hers was in her pocket for the same reason. He pulled the watch from his pocket, looked at it. "It's been almost six hours. Even crawling, we'd have been there by now."

"Do you think we got off course?"

He looked at her, and she could tell he had an idea but didn't want to say it.

"What, Alex? Come on, just tell me."

He sighed. "I don't think there is any military base. I think our friend at the store lied through his teeth."

Her heart sank to somewhere near the region of her stomach. "But why?"

"I don't know." He shook his head slowly. "Things have been hitting me for the past hour. Maybe my brain had to get baked before it started working properly,

Mel, but didn't it seem to you that all the stuff in that shop was awfully new? I mean, for an old rundown place like that, so far off the beaten track, shouldn't the stuff have been dusty? Even a little out of date?''

She blinked her eyes. They felt gritty. ''The water was rusty. As if…it hadn't been run in a long time. And the cooler, the one with the bottled water and soft drinks…looked brand new.''

Alex heaved a deep sigh. ''I'm sorry. I should have seen it. I mean, come on, it's a pretty unlikely coincidence that we just happened to wander into the one place where Katerina and Thomas had been. And I fell for it like a rookie. That old man sent us exactly where he wanted us to go.''

''He…sent us out here to die, didn't he?''

''Maybe. We're not gonna oblige him. There's no point in continuing. We need to think about turning back, Mel.''

She closed her eyes; the very thought of hiking another six hours back the way they had come was too painful to bear. She tried to hold her emotions in check, but they came bubbling out anyway. A sob broke first and her shoulders quaked and her breath hitched in her throat.

''Don't cry,'' Alex whispered, sliding his arms around her shoulders, pulling her close to his chest. ''You're wasting water.''

She tried to laugh, but it hurt too much. ''We aren't going to make it back, are we?''

''Sure we are.''

''We don't have enough water, Alex. You know that as well as I do. We don't have enough water.''

''All that means, honey, is that we'll be damn thirsty for the last few miles. But we *will* make it.''

She glanced up at the sky. "Maybe. Maybe if we wait until the sun goes down, walk during the night when it's cool."

"You're reading my mind."

She nodded. "How long till sundown?"

"Two hours, two and a half."

"We can't stay here. We need to find a better place to rest. We'll just bake if we stay here."

Nodding, Alex got to his feet, looking around. "There are some boulders and a few scrub trees over there."

"Any shade?"

"I'll let you know when we get there. Come on." He reached down a hand. She took it and let him pull her to her feet, every muscle in her body screaming in protest. She picked up the backpack, which she was beginning to hate with a passion that was utterly wasted on inanimate objects, and slung it over her shoulder. She swore she was getting sunburned right through her clothes.

"Lead the way," she said.

Alex shouldered his pack and started off. When they reached the spot, about two hundred grueling yards away, he sighed audibly. "I'm sorry. This is no shadier than where we were before."

"No," she said, looking around. "But it will be. Take off your pack, Alex. Rest a minute while I think about this." He did, setting his pack aside, watching her intently. Mel looked at what she had to work with. There were three boulders and two skinny, leafless trees. The boulders had their backs to the sun and cast a modicum of shade in front of each of them, but they were a few feet apart, so the fiery sun blasted in between them like a flame thrower.

"How far apart would you say the two closest rocks are at the top?" she asked Alex.

"I don't know. Four, five feet?"

"Can you break that dead tree off, do you think? As close to the base as possible?"

Alex nodded. "Maybe. I think so. Do you have some kind of a plan?"

"Yeah. Get me that tree. Snap off the branches."

Alex dug the pocket knife out of his pocket. He'd added it to their purchases at the store and wondered aloud if he would ever have call to use it. "I wonder if one of the blades has saw teeth." He went to the tree, knelt at its base, took hold with both hands and bent it.

The tree was only about two inches in diameter, but that was still tough to break with your bare hands, Mel thought. Yet she heard the cracking sounds that told her Alex was succeeding. She would have given her right arm for a small chain saw.

She left him to his work and took off her backpack, tossing it down, then she went to his and removed the sleeping bag, unrolling it, unzipping it. She looked around for scattered rocks, smaller ones, gathering them up into two piles, one in front of each boulder. Then she glanced back at Alex.

The tree had broken off except for some stringy, stubborn bits in the center that he was currently sawing at with the pocketknife. They finally gave way, and he took off his hat to swipe the sweat from his forehead, then got to his feet and snapped off the small dry branches. He piled the refuse in the center of the area, then brought the stripped-down tree over to her.

"Over here," she said, moving to the first boulder. "I need you to boost me up on top. Then hand up the tree. Okay? I'm gonna make us a curtain."

He looked at the boulder, then at her. "It's too hot up there. You'll burn your hands."

"It'll be fine."

"No. I'll go."

"I can't boost you up, Alex, you're too big."

"Try."

Sighing, she bent down and laced her fingers together.

"Not like that. Drop down on one knee. Pretend you're about to propose marriage."

"Oh, I get it. You'll be so eager to escape me that you'll fly up onto the boulder, right?"

He made a face. She dropped down on one knee, and he used the other as a step stool to boost himself onto the boulder. He sucked air through his teeth when he got to the top on all fours, and Mel knew his palms must be burning. He scrambled to his feet as fast as possible. "Okay, toss me up our curtain rod."

She did. He laid the pole across the two boulders, skinny end toward him and a good foot of it on the rock, with less of the other end balanced on the other boulder. "Now how do you suggest we keep it here?" he asked.

"I thought we could pile rocks around and over each end. Here." She picked up some of the stones she'd gathered, reaching up to him. Alex had to kneel on the sizzling-hot boulder to reach them, but he did it, then piled them carefully, until the pole was fairly secure. Then he jumped down, and they repeated the entire process on the other boulder.

Finally she handed him up the sleeping bag. He used the ties attached to one end of the sleeping bag to tie it to the pole. The other end had no ties, so he weighted it to the top of the boulder with a few of the rocks.

"Good thinking," Mel called, nodding approval.

Alex jumped down. A large pool of shade spread over the ground now. "You're one smart woman, you know that, Mel?"

She didn't answer. She wasn't smart. She'd done two years at a community college, and she worked at her mom's saloon. She didn't know what wine went with what meat, and she didn't know why anyone would want or need more than one fork to eat their dinner. She didn't know about foreign policy or opera or designer clothes or society rules. What's more, she didn't want to.

Sighing, she dragged her backpack closer. Then she lay down in the shady area, using it as a pillow.

Alex followed suit, stretching out beside her. "You want a drink?" he asked.

"Yes, desperately, but maybe we should save it."

"We won't be so thirsty at night. Go ahead." He managed to get the canteen off his backpack without getting up, removed the cap and held it out to her. She took a drink, fighting with herself and her need to gulp, just sipping, letting it soak into her lips and mouth and tongue before swallowing the precious fluid. Then she handed it back to him.

He took a small drink, too, then capped it and set it down.

"I love water," she said. "I don't know if I ever knew how much until right now. I think I preferred nearly drowning in the river to baking slowly in the heat."

"Yeah, me, too. Almost makes me wish I didn't live in a condo, so I could have my own pool."

She lifted her brows and turned her head sideways

on her makeshift pillow to study him in profile. "You live in an apartment?"

"Mmm-hmm. You sound surprised."

"I am. I guess I expected you to live in someplace like…like where we were staying. Lap of luxury."

"Well, it's a *nice* condo."

"But there's no pool?"

"There's a pool. A nice pool. Just not my own."

"Mm." She relaxed a little. The heat was drugging. "We have a pond. It's down the hill behind the house. You follow this path that meanders through a little copse of woods. Cool and shady woods. Green and moist all the time. The path leads to a small clearing, with this wild pond right in the middle of it." She sighed. "The water is so clear you can watch the fish swim by. The deer come out to drink just at dusk. They like the grass there, cause it's always new and tender. We mow it a few times a year to keep it from going to weed. If you get there before them and sit real quiet, you can watch them come out to graze and sip the cool water."

"No chlorine smell, I'll bet. No fellow tenants. No filter pump running to disturb the peace and quiet with its hum."

"The only things humming are the bees. And there are crickets whirring. And birds singing. Frogs croaking real deep just before dark. The fish jumping up to nab a passing mosquito and then splashing back into the water again. There's nothing like a wild pond in the dead of night. It's like something mystical. A whole world comes to life out there when the sun goes down."

His voice was slower, softer when he spoke again. "I want to go there with you, Mel. As soon as we get out of this mess. I want to see your magic pond."

"Maybe go for a swim?"

"So long as it won't bother the bullfrogs."

She smiled very softly, thinking about taking him there, to her favorite spot. Sharing it with him. She was thinking of slipping into that cool, clear water with Alex Stone when she fell asleep.

They found a building. It was a weathered, unpainted shack with a red gas pump in the front. And it was empty. Abandoned, but according to Wes and Mick Flyte, there were signs someone had been there recently. The dust on the shelves had been disturbed, as if items had been stacked on them and then removed again.

Selene knew it had been occupied, too, but her methods were less mundane. She felt the energy. "My sister has been here. Right here, in this building. I can still feel her."

"There was food, too," Wes said. "Can't you smell that? Some kind of meat. Ham, maybe a sandwich."

"There's water on the floor here, and a big square shape in the dust." Wes went to the back door, stepped out and came back in again. "Tire tracks out back," he said. "And boot tracks, lots of them. A number of men made several trips in and out of this building today."

Flyte shook his head. "So if this is where Alex called from, it was a setup. Someone here fed them, probably sold them supplies, told them to give me a location of fifty miles away and sent them out into the desert toward some nonexistent military base. Why?"

"So they would die out there?" Selene asked.

"No. I think they went to far too much trouble for something as simple as that," Wes said. "If they wanted them dead, why not just kill them here? They must have spotted them coming this way across the desert. They must have known this was the only building in the area and acted fast to make it look real. They wanted them out in that desert for a reason. We just don't know what it is yet.''

"I'd say it would be best for us to find them before that reason makes itself apparent," Mick Flyte said, yanking his phone from his pocket and punching buttons. "To hell with all this tiptoeing around. I'm going to get some choppers out here and see if we can find them before it's too late.''

Chapter 11

When Alex woke some time later, it was full dark. The darkest night he could imagine. He was lying on his side, with his arms wrapped around Mel and her body spooned so tightly with his that it was tough to tell where he ended and she began. The only parts of him that were warm were the parts that were touching her. His back was colder than midnight.

Mel rolled completely over, so she was facing him. She tucked her face against his neck and burrowed closer, and he automatically tightened his arms around her when she settled into comfort. He thought that was what she'd been doing for however long they'd been sleeping here—snuggling one side against him, then turning to warm the other side. God, he loved holding her this way, being this close to her. If she only knew how he felt whenever he touched her or looked at her, she would—

She lifted her chin, and her eyes blinked open, meeting his, still dazed with sleep. She laid her lips against his, and he knew she was only partly awake, but he really didn't care. He wanted to kiss her, needed to kiss her. He slid his hand up her back to cup her head, so he could cradle it and move it just so, and he moved his lips over hers, teasing them open. When they parted, he kissed her harder, deeper, seeking and taking all she would let him, and wanting more. And when she responded, his entire body came alive. It was a hungry kiss. It held all the heat the sun had baked into him throughout the day. He kissed her with his entire being, every part of him. His legs rubbed over hers, his hips pressed to hers, and his torso melded with hers while his arms held her close and his fingers tangled in her hair and his mouth explored. She was meeting and reacting to everything he did, coming awake and seeming to catch fire. Her body strained against his, her hands held him to her, and her mouth opened wide to receive him.

His heart pounded in his chest, and he could feel hers answering in kind. He couldn't catch his breath. She was panting, too. His mouth slid from hers, across her face, her jaw, to her ear.

"We were right to wait," a deep voice said from the darkness.

Beneath him, Melusine went utterly still.

Alex lifted his head away from her, staring down into her stunned eyes, as breathless as she was. Then he turned slowly toward the man's voice, and he saw not one man, but three. They stood in a rough semicircle, the desert night their backdrop, and each one held an automatic weapon pointed at the two of them.

"It's obvious now," the first man, the leader, went on. "The other two are mere imposters. Waiting, watching them, was the only way to know for sure. But there is no longer any doubt. These are the real Katerina and Thomas Barde.''

Mel's hand inched toward the gun. It was on the ground, right beneath her backpack. She'd tucked it there, as if tucking it under her pillow before lying down.

"Get to your feet," the man ordered. "Now, and keep your hands in front of you." He spoke with an accent, she noticed, but only a slight one. She couldn't identify it.

Alex got up and reached down to take her hand, pulling her to her feet with him, holding her close beside him.

"Get the packs," the man barked, and one of his two companions surged forward. He gripped a pack in each hand, hefted them and turned to take them back to the leader. Mel moved her foot carefully, pushing sand over the gun that lay just behind where she stood. She did it without looking down and hoped to the heavens she had covered it well enough to keep them from seeing it.

She was terrified and shivering—probably directly due to experiencing polar opposites of extreme emotion. First burning up in Alex's arms. Now frozen in absolute terror.

Alex glanced her way, frowned, reading in her face that she was up to something. His eyes warned her to be still, to comply.

"Search them," the leader said. He was the smallest man in the group. Thin and hard, with cruel angles in his face and jaw. His small dark eyes reminded Mel of a rat's eyes. Cold and assessing and wily.

The other two men came forward. One of them ran

his hands over Mel's arms, her legs, her torso, her buttocks, between her thighs, over her chest. He was thorough. She stood still, not fighting him. She resisted the urge to knee him between the legs when she knew perfectly well he was copping a feel. They were the ones with the weapons here. Now was not the time.

The one searching Alex found his handgun and took it from him. He tucked it into the back of his own pants—dark tan multipocketed pants and a matching shirt. It was a uniform of some kind.

"Good," the leader said. "Now, you two, come."

Alex took a single step forward.

"I...I can't," Mel said. She pressed a hand to her forehead, closed her eyes, prayed for the strength and acting skills to pull off her little ruse. "I'm just...too weak. Please..."

As Alex turned toward her in surprise and worry, she let her body go limp and slumped to the ground. Alex shot toward her, but stopped when the leader shouted at him to be still. Then he looked at Mel. "My dear Katerina, you did not seem so weakened when we arrived. But it's of little consequence to me. You can get up, or I can kill you where you lie. I'll leave the decision to you."

She shoved the tiny handgun down the back of her jeans even as she made a show of struggling to get to her feet. The tail of the khaki button-down shirt hung over her hips, hiding the bulge, she hoped. She walked weakly. Alex put his arm around her to help her.

The leader started off across the desert, and they followed. They had little choice, with the other two following behind, prodding them with guns if they slowed at all. She hoped to God they didn't have to walk far. Rest had only given her limbs time to stiffen. Now they moved like hinges sorely in need of oil. Slowly, under protest, creaking with pain. She wondered how the hell she and Alex were going to beat these three morons senseless when it hurt this much just to walk.

Over a slight rise, she saw two vehicles, older model SUVs, tan and brown. She and Alex were hustled into the back seat of one of them. The leader and one of the gunmen got into the front. The third man drove the other one, following behind.

Mel slid closer to Alex as the vehicle bounded over the impossible terrain. She curled against him, and he put his arm around her protectively. "Try not to be afraid, Mel. We're just biding our time, waiting for the right moment. I'm damned sure not going to let anything happen to you," he whispered.

"Neither am I." She reached behind her to clasp his hand where it rested and slid it lower over her bottom, until he could feel the hard outline of the gun she'd tucked there. His eyes shot to hers, then warmed.

"Have I told you you're one of a kind?" he asked her softly.

"No talking," the driver barked.

"I don't understand," Selene whispered. She sat beside Mick Flyte in a helicopter that swooped over the barren wasteland below in search of people. Wes was on the ground, trying to pick up some trace of Alex and Mel from closer range and connected to Selene by radio. She wore a headset and spoke into the microphone that hovered a few inches from her face. "There's nothing. It's as if they just disappeared. God, where could they be?"

"Wait, I see something!" Mick said. He pointed

briefly, then swung the chopper expertly to the left and lower. "What is that?"

"I don't know. A…a tent?"

The radio crackled in her ear. "What?" Wes asked. "What do you see? Is it them?"

"No. No, I don't see any people, but there's something," Selene told him. "It's about three hundred yards north, I think, of where you are."

"Are you hovering over it?" The question crackled back at her.

"Yes. Can you see us?"

"Yeah, I'm on the way. Stay right there."

Soon the vehicle Wes had been driving came bounding and bouncing over the uneven ground toward the spot below them. It came to a rough stop in front of the olive-green square below, and only then did Mick Flyte set the chopper down.

Selene tugged the headpiece off and jumped from the open chopper, bending low and squinting in the blade-driven sandstorm as she ran until she was clear. She spotted Wes, looking at the contraption and shaking his head slowly. "They're not here. But I think they were."

Selene looked past him at the sleeping bag rigged up to provide shade, and the marks of feet in the sand.

"There are tire tracks over that way," Wes said softly. "And where the ground isn't packed too hard to hold them, there are footprints. Three sets coming this way from the tire tracks, five sets going back."

"You mean…?"

"The little store was a setup, we already guessed as much. The man who gave them directions was probably one of the bad guys. He sent them out here far enough so they'd be worn out, weak and exhausted by the time his counterparts arrived to pick them up."

"Less of a struggle that way," Mick Flyte muttered. "And no chance of witnesses."

His voice, coming from so close behind her, startled Selene. She hadn't even heard his approach.

"There's no way in hell we can know where they might have taken them," Wes said softly.

"There are ways," Flyte told him. "Don't you doubt it, there are ways. We'll get a plaster cast of the tire marks, find out what kind of vehicle they fit that could also handle this terrain and put out a description. And we can fill this desert with men, scour every inch of it.

"By then they could be dead." Wes sounded grim, and though he looked at Selene, he kept speaking to the other man. "You do what you can, Mr. Flyte. Follow your protocol and bring in your experts. We have our own contingency plan in situations like this."

Selene knew exactly what he meant.

Flyte lifted his brows. "Contingency plan? And just what is this plan, Mr. Brand?"

"Call in the family," Wes said softly.

"The *whole* family," Selene said with a firm nod.

They had been blindfolded ten minutes into the ride. They were taken from the vehicle, blind, stumbling and helpless. Alex didn't know for sure when to make a move but sensed the time wasn't right just yet. He would know when it was. Or so he told himself. When the damp cloth that smelled of ether was crushed over his nose and mouth, he had second thoughts. He told himself not to breathe, heard the sudden sounds of Mel struggling, then relaxing as the ether took her. And then he was gone, too.

When he came to, he had to blink for several minutes before his vision cleared and his eyes adjusted to the dimness. The only source of light came through the barred window of a heavy-looking wooden door that stood directly across from him. There was a hard floor beneath him. The wall he leaned against felt like it was built of cinder blocks. It braced him up in a sitting position, and there was a warm body lying limp across his outstretched legs.

Blinking away the grogginess, trying hard to focus his mind, he felt softness beneath his hand and realized two things. First, that he was no longer blindfolded, and second, that his fingers were buried in soft, short hair. He bent over Mel where she lay, lifting her up off his legs by her shoulders, only to see her head loll forward, limp and doll-like. "Mel. Wake up, honey, come on."

"She'll be all right," a man's accented voice said. "She's smaller than you. The ether takes longer to wear off on a small woman."

Jerking his head to the left, Alex realized for the first time that he and Mel were not alone in this dank cell. He peered through the darkness. "Who are you?"

"I am…" The man looked toward the barred door, cut himself off. "We are the first couple these criminals mistook for Thomas and Katerina Barde. You, apparently, are the second."

"We?" The man's face was becoming clearer, as Alex's vision adjusted to the dimness and the gas wore off. The man was sitting on the floor, a woman huddled close beside him. He was nodding toward Mel now. "It's amazing, the resemblance."

"I don't really see it, myself," the woman said, her voice soft. She got to her feet and came closer, leaning over Mel and gently pushing her hair from her face. "Poor thing. She's going to have such a pounding headache when she wakes. At least, I did when I woke."

It was her. It was Katerina herself, Alex realized. She was somehow dimmer than her press had made her seem. Or maybe it was that she was tired and dirty, dressed in tattered rags, her hair oily and limp.

"Who are you?" Thomas Barde asked Alex, coming closer before sitting down again, so that they could speak in whispers.

"I'm Alex Stone. This is Melusine Brand. We've been impersonating you in order to help avoid an international incident. Of course, that was when the powers that be were still working under the assumption that you two had run off together on a whim. No one realized you'd been abducted."

"They were going to use us to gain control of our country—and then just kill us," Katerina whispered, sinking to the floor to sit again beside her husband. He put his arm around her shoulders and squeezed her close to his side. Her head was lowered, her eyes, Alex thought, damp. "But they overheard us quarreling. That alone wouldn't have saved us, I'm certain. Except that only a few hours later, someone, one of their despicable spies, I assume, showed them footage of the two of you. Rather…intimate footage."

Alex wondered when it had been taken. He tried to picture himself and Mel together, and realized that, to outside eyes, they must seem intimate most of the time. He was always finding excuses to touch her. She was always looking up at him with those eyes….

He blinked the thoughts away, told himself to focus on the present conversation. "So they decided that you two must be the imposters," Alex said. "And that we were the real couple."

Katerina shook her head, her motions jerky. "It confused them enough so that they put all plans on hold until they could determine which was the genuine couple. But it doesn't matter anymore. Now they have all four of us. And I have no doubt that just as soon as they figure out which of us are the real Bardes…''

"They're not going to figure that out," Alex promised. "That part of this is entirely within our control. We aren't going to give it up."

"Then what's to stop them from simply killing us all?" Katerina whispered. She closed her eyes, lowered her head to her husband's shoulder and wept softly.

"They do not want to kill Katerina. They want to use her as leverage against her father," Alex said.

"They've taped enough footage of us to convince Belisle we're still alive for several weeks to come," Thomas said very softly. "They have no reason to keep any of us alive for much longer."

"Then my suggestion would be that we find a way to get the hell out of here as soon as possible." Mel moaned and lifted her head from where it rested on Alex's shoulder. He touched her face, smoothed her hair. "It's okay, I know it hurts. Come on, wake up now."

Her eyes blinked open, then squeezed closed again. "Oh, God, I feel like I've been on a three-day drunk."

"It'll get better. Try to breathe nice and deep."

She inhaled nasally, then scrunched up her face. "Gawd, it stinks in here. Smells like a stinkbug crawled up a skunk's ass and died. What *is* that?"

Katerina's head came up, and she blinked at Mel in what looked like amazement. "*She* impersonated *me?*" she asked softly.

Mel squinted at her. "Damn, you're her, aren't you?"

"It's probably best we don't talk too much about

who's who just now, hon,'' Alex told her as she sat up more fully. The act took her out of his arms and left him chilled. She leaned back against the cinder block wall and pushed her hands up over her face and forehead, then back through her hair, closing her eyes again. It was as if she were trying to push the ache from her head. Then she went stiff, and her eyes widened. She drove her hand behind her, feeling her bottom, sighing in apparent relief as she shot Alex a look.

He read the look loud and clear. The gun was still there. They hadn't found it.

''I should give it to you,'' she whispered, her hand dipping down the back of her khaki pants. ''You're probably going to be more effective with it than me.'' She glanced quickly at Katerina and amended, ''Uh, than I, I mean.''

He slid closer, pressing his side to hers, sliding one hand behind his back to take the gun from her. Then he slid it into the back of his own pants.

''What are you doing?'' Thomas asked. ''Do you have a—'' he dropped his voice to the barest whisper ''—weapon?''

Alex nodded.

''You mustn't do anything to anger these people,'' Katerina pleaded softly, her eyes welling with tears. ''They're dangerous. Don't upset them, whatever you do, or they'll kill us.''

''Upset them?'' Mel asked, fixing her eyes on the frightened woman. ''Hey, Miss Manners, these men intend to put us all into the ground, in case you're not clear on that. They're going to kill us no matter how polite and cooperative we might be.'' She looked at Alex. ''Have you explained this to them?''

''Of course we know all of that.'' Katerina bit her

lip, shook her head. "But it would be rash to act on our own. We simply have to be patient, be calm. We should do everything they ask of us until help arrives. And it *will* arrive. Even now, there must be a massive rescue attempt underway. Someone will come for us anytime now. Surely they will."

Mel looked at the woman in disbelief. "You can be patient and do what you're told and wait for someone to come save you, if that's what you think best. From what I understand, that's pretty much what they teach women in your country to do, anyway, isn't it? Be patient and do as they're told? As for me, I'm gonna fight my way out of here or die trying."

"I do not care what you think of my country. That does not give you the right to make decisions here that could be the ruin of all of us!" Katerina cried, and she was loud this time, loud enough to attract attention from outside.

"This is America sweetie. Around here, I have just as many rights as you do."

A face appeared at the bars. "Silence!"

Katerina crowded against her husband, hiding her face, shaking all over.

The guard retreated, and in the distance Alex heard him telling someone they were awake. Then there were more steps returning to the door. Keys jangled and scraped in the lock, and the cell door opened. Three men stepped inside, two of them dangling handcuffs from their fingers. "On your feet, and hold your arms out."

Katerina and Thomas were up, offering their wrists to the handcuffs instantly. Mel said, "Screw you," and stayed where she was, on the floor. Alex rolled to his feet, but only to plant them in front of Mel.

One guard cuffed Thomas and Katerina, and led them out of the cell. The other came nose to nose with Alex. "Your hands, sir."

Alex reached behind him for the gun.

Mel jumped to her feet, elbowing him in the process and then nodding toward the hall beyond the open door when she caught his eye. He saw them then. A line of men with automatic weapons.

"Fine, cuff us," Mel said. "But know that you are going to be very, very sorry you treated us this way. More sorry than you can even imagine." She stuck her wrists out, thinking about what her mother and sisters, and Wes Brand, were going to do to these bastards when they caught up to them.

Alex held his hands out, too, reluctantly, but in the end surrendering. It was still not the right time.

They were cuffed and led down a cool gray hall made of cinder blocks. The light fixtures overhead were wire-caged bulbs dangling from aging wire. The two of them were placed in a small room in two hard-backed chairs. Another bulb hung in there, and nothing else. The door was closed, locked.

"They'll be listening," Alex whispered. "It's standard. Leave us alone awhile, see if we say anything revealing."

"They want revealing, I'll give them revealing," Mel said. "You guys are not going to live very long. Because my family is going to come over here and kick your ever-loving asses all the way back to wherever the hell you came from."

The door opened a half hour later. Mel had spent the entire time talking about the numerous ways in which the men responsible for this were going to suffer, while

Alex had spent the entire time warning her to keep quiet. She didn't care. She wanted to piss them off. You pissed a man off, he would lose his temper, just as sure as night followed day. And when a man lost his temper, he could be outsmarted.

A man came in, puffing on a big fat cigar, pacing the floor in front of them. "You are very wise," he said to Alex. Then he sent a narrow-eyed glare at Mel. "And you are very sure of your father's reach and his power. Overconfident, I would say."

"I really don't care what you would say," she said. "But you might be interested in what Freud would have to say about the way you're sucking on that cigar."

He laughed softly, shrugged. "Amusing." He'd gone a bit red in the face, though. Good. He closed the door, locked it from the inside with a key, then dropped the key back into the pocket of his green camouflage shirt. "Your names," he demanded, turning to face them, walking toward them until he stood right in front of them.

They were alone in the room with a guard outside the door. The key was in this man's pocket. Mel could see Alex's sharp eyes taking in every detail, analyzing, plotting, weighing the odds. God, she found that attractive, that sharp mind of his.

"Your names," the man said again.

"Sonny and Cher," Mel snapped. "What, you don't recognize us?"

The man drew back his hand and smacked her so fast she never saw it coming—a swift backhand across the face that snapped her head to one side. Alex surged to his feet, but the man was expecting that. He had a gun in his other hand, and he pressed the barrel to Alex's forehead and used it to shove him back into his chair.

"Your names," the man repeated.

Mel touched her split lip with her tongue, looked the jerk in the eye. "He's Donny, and I'm Marie. Haven't you seen our show?"

He came toward her to hit her again, but she stuck her feet out and tripped him so he landed face first on the floor. Alex sprang fast, kneeling on the guy's back, wrapping the chain of his cuffs around his throat and pulling tight to cut off the flow of blood giving oxygen to his brain.

"I lied," Mel said, leaning close, just before the guy's eyes closed. "He's Batman, and I'm Robin."

The fat man passed out. Or died, she wasn't sure which and didn't particularly care. "The son of a bitch hit me," she muttered.

Alex got off him and rolled him over, patted him down and found the handcuff keys. Then he unlocked Mel's cuffs and searched her face. "Are you all right?"

"That son of a bitch *hit* me." This time she punctuated it by giving the big lump a good swift kick in the ribs. "Try that when I'm not handcuffed, you fat bastard," she muttered. Then she met Alex's concerned eyes. "Yes, I'm all right. I'm royally pissed, but I'm all right." She took the keys from him and unlocked his cuffs. He touched her lip where she was bleeding.

Alex located a microphone, barely concealed in the light fixture, and crushed it. "I'm sorry I couldn't stop him."

"He looks pretty stopped to me."

Alex pulled the gun from his waistband and handed Mel the weapon he'd taken from the fat slob on the floor. They went to the door, and Alex used the key to unlock it, then opened it just a crack, peered out, closed it again.

"Well?" she asked, watching his face, trying to read their chances there.

"One guard, armed, just to the left. Another one standing in front of another door, just across the hall. That's probably where they have the other two. That's all I can see from here."

She nodded, holding her gun ready. "I'll take the one across the hall," she said. "You take the one beside the door."

Alex paused to look at her with a frown. "If I didn't know better, I'd almost think you were enjoying this."

"I'll enjoy it more when we're out of here."

"Yeah, I'm with you on that one. On three, okay?"

She nodded, took a breath.

"One, two…" On three, Alex yanked open the door and clocked the guard upside the head with the butt of his handgun. The one across the hall reached for his weapon, but Mel had hers a foot from his nose before he could do much harm. She pressed a forefinger to her lips to tell him to be silent, then took his gun away and herded him into the room she and Alex had been in. Alex dragged the unconscious guard inside, as well, then looked at the frightened conscious one. "Sorry about this," he said, and nailed the guy just as he had the other one. The guard looked briefly surprised, then slumped to the floor.

"Now what?" Mel asked, closing the door behind them after glancing up and down the hall to be sure they hadn't been seen. Alex was handcuffing the two guards, hands behind their backs, not in front as Alex and Mel had been cuffed.

Then he returned to the door, opened it and looked out. "The door across the hall is still closed. We have

to assume that's where they are, and that there's someone in there questioning them, as well."

"So what do we do?" She was whispering, just as
he had been, in case someone, somewhere, was listening
in.

"We go in there and get our counterparts, and then
we get the hell out of here."

"That door is probably locked like this one was. How
are we going to get them to open it?"

Alex shrugged. "We could try knocking." He strode
across the hall, rapped twice on the door. Mel locked
the door of the room they had been in and closed it
behind her as she hurried to follow Alex.

Muttering, the man inside, who had no doubt been
questioning Katerina and Thomas just as Alex had surmised, unlocked the door and opened it. He was greeted
by a fist to the face. The guy went down hard on his
back, his head landing right at Thomas's feet. Thomas
hauled off and kicked the man repeatedly.

"All right, all right, he's out," Alex whispered, as
he and Mel rushed into the room.

"He should be dead," Thomas growled. "You leave
his kind alive, they only come back to attack you again
later. Kill him. This is war."

Alex shook his head, and Mel knew it was too late
to warn the couple to be quiet. "That's not war," Alex
said. "That's murder. Now come on." Using the key
he'd pocketed, he unfastened Thomas's handcuffs, then
tossed the keys to Mel. She unlocked Katerina's cuffs.

"You're going to get us all killed," Katerina whispered, tears streaming down both cheeks.

Thomas took the gun from the fallen man, and the
four of them crept into the hall, locking the door from

the inside and pulling it closed behind them. Not that Mel thought it was going to fool anyone at this point.

The hall was long, windowless, with doors at either end. They knew that beyond one door were stairs leading downward, deeper into the earth, because that was the one they had come through from their cell to this area. Alex led them toward the far end of the hall and the other door. Another hallway crossed the one they traversed. They crept through the intersection, and Mel realized she was holding her breath. God, she was scared. And alive, more alive, she thought, than she had ever been. It occurred to her that Alex had been right. She *was* enjoying this somehow, somewhere far beneath the fear. Sneaking through an underground bunker filled with killers, carrying a gun, rescuing a princess. Even if she was a spoiled and whiny little princess. Hell, Mel thought, she might just love this. If they survived, anyway.

"I'm sick," she muttered. "Sick."

"It's just the stress," Alex whispered. "Try to hold on, hon, we'll be out of here soon."

He called her "hon." She loved that, too.

They reached the door, opened it, saw a set of stairs leading upward and took them. At the top, another hall led to a door with natural light shining in around the edges. It had to lead to the outside. Mel's heart beat faster.

They ran toward that door, and then all stopped, crowded around it, breathless with anticipation. Alex gripped the knob, turned it.

"Unlocked," he whispered.

He pushed the door open very slowly, then peered outside. Mel crowded closer to him, so she could see outside, as well. There were outbuildings, but they seemed lifeless, dead. There was a low stone wall, where some building had been started, but never finished. But there were no people. There were no guards. No one in sight at all. And there was a helicopter resting in the distance.

Chapter 12

Alex skimmed their surroundings. It was late afternoon, but full light. The sun hung low in the sky, painting it in brushstrokes of gold, orange and red. And the terrain here looked less desertlike than before. There were rocky hillsides and scraggly vegetation dotting the landscape.

The place appeared to have been some kind of storage facility at one time. A handful of barn-size structures stood in a half circle. Crumbling now, abandoned—or they had been until these jokers had taken up residence. He didn't know where the hell they were, or in what direction safety might lie. But he did know one thing. He knew he could fly that helicopter. Probably. Mick had given him a few informal lessons on his own chopper, back when they'd worked together in the Secret Service. The one outside wasn't exactly the same, but similar enough that he might just be able to get it off the ground.

Was it worth the risk?

Hell, they were facing certain death here. At least in the chopper they would have a chance. And a chance was all they needed.

"What's the plan?" Mel whispered from close beside him.

At his shoulder. He liked that about her. She didn't cower behind him the way Katerina cowered behind Thomas. She stood beside him. He had no doubt he could count on her in a pinch. She'd proven it often enough over the past few days.

He glanced down at her. "The chopper," he whispered. He nodded toward the only visible guard he'd been able to spot. The man was silhouetted in a glassless window, in the peak of the building off to the left. His head swung slowly from left to right as he scanned the area, keeping watch. Alex picked up the pattern, the cadence of his movements. "Crouch low and run to the helicopter quick as you can when I say go."

Mel turned to the two behind her, repeated his whispered command.

"Ready?" he asked.

"Ready."

He watched the guard, facing their building, gaze sliding like a shadow over it. Then he was scanning the opposite direction. "Go!" Alex whispered.

They ran, bent low, silently, scurrying like bugs when the lights came on. Alex reached the chopper first and helped the others in, one by one. He climbed in last. "Get down low. Now!" he whispered.

They all crouched down in the chopper. The guard turned slowly...and saw nothing.

Alex knew it was only a matter of minutes, seconds maybe, before the interrogators and guard dogs he'd left bound and unconscious inside would come around and start stirring up a commotion. He examined the panel, the controls, his heart pounding so hard he swore it was audible to the others as he dug down deep for the knowledge he needed to get this thing in the air.

"Can you fly this thing, Alex?" Mel asked, her voice very low, a little shaky.

"We're about to find out." He licked his lips, nodded firmly. "Yeah, I think I can." Glancing at the other two, he said, "Get your weapons ready. The second I start this thing, they're going to come out shooting. I'll need a few seconds to get us off the ground. You're going to need to hold them off."

Mel caught his eyes, her own wide. "Should we...shoot to kill?"

"Aim for the torso. Less chance of missing."

She nodded, but he saw the look of uncertainty in her eyes.

"If it makes you feel better, don't think of it as trying to kill them. Think of it as trying to stop them from killing us. We'll send help back for them the minute we're safe."

She met his eyes, and the resolve in her own hardened and held. "They're not giving us much of a choice." She looked at the gun in her hand, it was bigger than the little .38 she'd had before, a semi-automatic, not a revolver. She checked it, flipped off the safety. She'd said she wasn't used to an automatic, but she seemed to know her way around the piece just fine.

Then she glanced at the other two. "Katerina, you get in the middle and stay down low."

Alex pulled out his own gun, checked Mel, saw her

with hers in her hand, her eyes dilated by adrenaline and skimming the compound.

"Let's do it, then. I'm a fair shot," she said. "You, Thomas?"

"I've won trophies for my marksmanship," he told her.

"Then you take the tower guy and I'll cover the door," Mel told him. She shot Alex a look. "You focus on the chopper. And don't worry, I've got your back. Just get us out of here."

He nodded once, flipped on the switches and hit the start button. The chopper came to life, motor humming more loudly than he had expected it to.

Behind him, Thomas's gun went off. But return fire came from the tower, pinging off the metal just above Alex's head.

Mel spun, aimed, fired, hitting the guard dead center of the chest and knocking him backward and out of sight.

The blades were beginning to turn, painstakingly slow, like tired old men walking up a long flight of stairs.

Another guard appeared in the window of the second outbuilding, looked toward them, frowning. The blades moved a little faster. A couple more seconds.

Mel's gun went off again just as the guard shouldered his rifle.

Alex saw him go down. Damn, she did have his back.

"Hurry, Alex," she said, turning toward the main building and firing three times. Then Thomas joined in. Alex turned to see a dozen men spilling from the open door of the building from which the four of them had just escaped, all armed, their weapons spitting fire. Alex pulled out his own gun to help. It sounded as if the chopper were in a hailstorm. Three men lay on the ground, and before Alex could even take aim, Mel dropped another.

"Thomas, aim before you shoot! You're just wasting ammo!" she shouted, and popped another.

She was freaking amazing. The blades were whirring now. Alex fired off two rounds, then took them airborne as fast as he could manage. The chopper leaned to one side, then the other, as he fought to remember his lessons. He got a feel for the stick, but they were still being hit by gunfire. Finally he got the thing moving more efficiently. Seconds later they were out of range of the men shooting at them from the ground.

Mel whooped a victory cry. "We did it," she said. "By God, we did it! We got away!"

Alex glanced at her. Damned if she wasn't glowing. "You're one hell of a shot, Melusine Brand."

"You're damn straight I am."

Their gazes locked for just an instant, and there was something there, something between them. Unspoken, unexamined, but real. He felt it right to his toes. If it wouldn't have meant crashing and burning, he would have kissed her right then. Long and hard. The urge to say to hell with the controls and do it anyway was almost too insistent to resist.

"Is that a radio?" Thomas asked, pointing at the headset that dangled from a hook near Alex's head.

"Looks like." He put the thing on, spent a few seconds locating the controls, and then turned knobs until he heard crackling in his ears. He found the frequency dial, then turned it until the digital panel showed him the emergency channel he and Mick had used in the old days. "Mayday, Mayday," he said. "Mick if you're listening, we're in a chopper, and we're safe. We have picked up the package, but we're being pursued." He glanced around them, shouting landmarks into the mike, having no clue if any of them were unique enough to help anyone find them.

A red light came on, and a deep-throated hum buzzed intermittently, like a persistent alarm clock. Alex looked at the gauges. "Hell, we didn't need this."

"What is it?" Thomas asked from behind him.

"They hit the fuel tank. We're going down." He met Mel's eyes. "I'm sorry. I tried."

"Tried and succeeded. You got us out of there, Alex. And we're not dead yet," she told him. "We're far from down for the count."

"There are parachutes back here!" Thomas yelled.

"How many?" Alex glanced back to see the man already strapping Katerina into one of them.

"Two," Thomas answered.

Alex nodded, manning the stick, trying to keep them in the air as long as possible, to steer them as far away from the compound as he could manage. He had no doubt those men were in pursuit, even now. He hadn't seen any other choppers on the ground, but there had been vehicles. Plenty of them.

"Two 'chutes," he repeated. "That's enough for the women. Mel, you and Katerina have to jump. I'll try to ditch this thing as far from you as possible. They'll follow the chopper. With any luck, they won't even see you two go down. I'll try to lead them away, give you plenty of time to get to safety. Or at least get hidden."

She stared him dead in the eye. "You're kidding, right?"

"Look off to the right. That looks like a town off that way. As soon as you get to the ground, get out of the 'chutes and head for it. It can't be more than a couple of miles.''

Mel put her hand over his on the stick. "I'm not going anywhere, Alex. If you think I am, then you haven't been paying much attention over the past few days. But I think you have been, and I think you know me a little bit better than you're pretending right now.''

"It's just as well," Thomas said from behind. "Because I have no intention of remaining in this contraption only to crash. I didn't survive this ordeal only to die in an ill-conceived escape attempt.''

Alex turned again, this time to see Thomas strapping on his own 'chute. "You son of a—''

"I'm sorry, Alex. You must understand, I am needed. It is vital to the security of the entire world that both Katerina and I survive this. Good luck—to both of you.''

Alex lifted his gun, but Mel put her hand over it, held it down. "Don't. Just let them go, Alex.''

Before she finished the sentence, Thomas had wrapped his arms around his wife and pushed them both out the side. Katerina's shriek of terror was quickly drowned out by the buzzing alarm and the sound of the coughing motor.

As the couple plummeted, Alex and Mel watched. He muttered to himself, "Not yet, not yet, not yet," as they fell. Thomas must have had some experience skydiving, because they waited long enough. Katerina's 'chute blossomed first, like a fat yellow flower. Thomas continued to plummet, but veering away from her; then his opened, as well. They floated slowly, safely, to the ground, hitting hard, Alex bet, maybe even breaking a limb or two if they weren't lucky. But they landed, and they were alive.

"They made it," Mel said.

Alex pushed the chopper to higher speeds, angling away from the pair on the ground, while Mel reached to the spot where Thomas and Katerina had been crouching behind them. "At least he left us the gun," she said, facing front again, the weapon in her hand. Then she sighed. "That arrogant bastard used up all the ammo. No wonder he left it. Not that it would have done him much good, anyway, with an aim like that. Trophies for marksmanship my ass."

"You should have let me point mine at his freaking face and force him to let you have the other parachute."

Mel shook her head slowly. "I wouldn't have gone either way. Come on, Alex, face it. You need me."

"You think so?" He stole a glance at her from the corner of his eye, while struggling to keep them aloft.

"I'm ten times more helpful than Thomas Barde would ever be in a fight," she told him.

"That's the understatement of the century." He swallowed hard. "I can't think of anyone else I'd rather have beside me when the chips are down, Mel," he said, his tone more serious. "I mean that."

She smiled a little. "Not even the princess?"

"You mean the simpering, spoiled, airhead?"

That made her smile even more, and the fact that she was bantering with him instead of leaning out the side retching while the chopper swung and bounded through the air made him admire her even more than he already had, if that were possible. He hadn't thought it was.

He took the chopper as far as he dared, until the choking and gasping of the engine made it clear he was risking a deadly crash. "Hold on, Mel. I'm gonna try to set us down. It's gonna be rough."

She did hold on—to him.

They hit hard, bounced up and hit again. The chopper tipped over onto one side, hurling Alex to the ground. Mel landed on top of him, and he braced, knowing damn well that if the chopper continued to roll, they could easily be crushed within the next couple of seconds.

But they weren't. The blades ground to a halt in the earth, holding the helicopter poised above them like a lean-to. Dust rose, thick and choking. He couldn't see. He felt Mel with his hands—her shoulders, arms, her face and neck. "Are you all right?"

She nodded, her chin moving on his chest. "I think so."

"Can you get up?"

"Maybe, if I knew which way up was."

She rose to her knees, and he managed to get to his beside her. The open side of the chopper was right above them.

Mel started to crawl out from under the beast, toward the front, but Alex gripped her hand. "No, not that way. The only thing holding it up is that blade. If it gives, it'll crush you."

"Well, we wouldn't want that."

"No," he said. "No, we sure as hell wouldn't." He released her hand and climbed into the upturned machine. He gripped the seats, climbed them like a ladder, toward the opening at the passenger side, which was facing almost straight up. Then he got himself anchored and reached back down to pull Mel up after him. When she joined him on the outside, perched atop the thing, he picked what he thought was the safest direction, squinting through the dust to look for debris and hazards. Seeing none, he nodded. They jumped to the ground, hand in hand, both stumbling when they landed. Alex helped Mel to her feet.

She sighed her relief, brushed some of the dirt off herself. "We made it."

"So far so good," he said. He took her hand again, and they walked slowly away from the wrecked helicopter.

She said, "You know, if I had to be kidnapped by international terrorists, there's no one else I'd rather have by my side, either."

"Yeah? Not even one of your cowboy cousins?"

"Not even," she told him. "As a matter of fact, you're starting to grow on me." Her hand squeezed his. "You're pretty amazing, Alex. For a city boy, I mean."

"Well, you're pretty amazing yourself. For an obnoxious little redneck."

"Thanks."

"You're welcome."

The dust thinned. They walked farther, blinking, wiping their eyes as the sunlight grew brighter, slanting right in at them. Gradually the dust dissipated enough so they could see their surroundings.

Six men became visible, forming a half circle around them, pointing weapons at them. The leader clapped his hands in slow applause. "Well done, my friends! *Very* well done. I think it's clear now who the real Bardes are. You two started all of this. You have the pride of kings, and you fight like warriors. You shouldn't have thought we could be fooled by those plain clothes you donned while your imposters dressed in finery." He looked around. "Where are they?"

"We dropped them over the nearest town. They're safely away from you."

The man shrugged. "No matter. We have no use for

them now. You, on the other hand, are too much trouble to keep around any longer.''

''You can't ransom us if we're dead,'' Mel told him. ''My father's not a fool. He'll require proof that I'm still alive before he gives in to anything you might demand.''

''Don't be silly. Of course he's a fool. Otherwise he wouldn't let his daughter traipse about the world putting herself at risk, while he remains safe in his presidential palace.''

He came closer to them. ''Do you know who I am, Katerina Barde?''

She shook her head slowly.

''No, of course you don't. Your father doesn't trust you with anything more important than looking beautiful and behaving like royalty. My name is Curnyn. I'm the leader of the Tantillan Revolutionary Army.''

''It's not an army. It's barely a terrorist organization. In fact, pressed to define you, I'd go with the term 'band of thugs.'''

He smiled at her. *Smiled.* ''You have been a worthy opponent, Katerina Barde. It's been a privilege playing this game against you.'' He glanced at Alex. ''Both of you. There's no honor in defeating a weakling. But you two—you've given me a grand chase, a delightful challenge.''

''You haven't defeated us yet, Curnyn.''

He drew a breath, pursed his lips, lowered his head. ''Sadly, I have, princess. The game is at an end. I have plenty of videotape. More than enough to convince your father that you are alive and extract all I want from him. So, I win. And you…you will be killed by firing squad at dawn.''

He nodded to his men, who rushed forward.

Alex fought, and he saw with pride that Mel got in a few good blows, too, but they were outnumbered and soon subdued by force, their arms pulled behind their backs and handcuffed.

Wes sat on the parched ground, with his back straight and his legs crossed. He was silent, his eyes slightly closed, his every sense open and waiting for some hint of his missing cousin. He put her face in his mind's eye. Focused on her laugh, the sound of her voice, the light in her eyes, the touch of her hand. The more thoroughly he could paint her image in his mind, in all his senses, the more likely he would be able to connect to her essence and get some clue of where she was right now.

Behind him, groups of men talked, planned and organized. Teams were forming around huge maps that wrestled with the wind. They'd intercepted a radio message a short while ago, believed to be from Alex. He had given a few landmarks before they had lost contact with him. The experts agreed he had been calling from a helicopter. It wasn't a trick or a lie to throw them off. The sounds in the background had been authentic. Coming from a real chopper. One they had been unable to raise since, much less locate by radar, which did not bode well.

Wes had asked Selene to keep everyone off his back for a few minutes. To give him some quiet time. She understood, the way very few other people would have, and she was doing a terrific job of it, too, right up until the rumble of more vehicles broke into his mind, and his senses told him the *other* troops had arrived.

He opened his eyes. Garrett was just getting out of a pickup truck that had to be a rental, his wife Chelsea beside him. Cousin Luke and pretty Jasmine got out the other side. Beautiful Taylor climbed out of the back, her long raven hair catching a breeze, dancing in it. Her eyes found Wes's without much of a hunt, and he stopped naming the other Brands who were debarking from a half dozen other vehicles. He knew they had all come. Of course they had. That was what Brands did.

Wes got to his feet, met Taylor halfway and folded her into his arms. God, it felt good to hold her again this way. It was beyond him how a man could love a woman so much that it physically hurt to be away from her, but that was exactly how he felt about his wife. "Where's Wolf?" he asked her.

"*Michael* is at the Texas Brand," she told him, faking a stern tone of voice that was blown by the smile in her eyes. "Sarah and Jake came in from New Orleans late last night. They let us talk them into staying at the house to do child-care duty. Marcus and Casey are joining them there, too."

He lifted a brow. "Any particular reason you all chose Marcus and Sarah as the Brands to stay behind?"

She slanted a glance up at him. "These Oklahoma girls are Marcus and Sarah's half sisters. I'm not even sure all of them realize it yet." She shook her head. "Chelsea thought we should get the high drama out of the way before we reunited them. And I agree with that."

"So do I," Wes said. "So do you think the four of them can handle the baby Brands?"

"Vidalia stayed behind, as well. I tend to think she could handle all eight of them by herself, if necessary."

"Eight?" He counted mentally. There was little Bubba, and Maria-Michelle, Ben's boy, Zachary, Luke's son, Baxter, and Elliot's baby girl, Montoya, who was exactly the same age as his own precious Michael "Wolf" Brand. But that was only six.

"Mel's sister has twins, don't forget. Little Dahlia and C.C. can't be left out."

"Right. Eight. Land sakes, we're creating a dynasty here."

They shared a smile, one that quickly turned serious. "Everyone else is here, hon. We want to help. What can we do?"

Wes looked around and saw that, indeed, his four brothers, Garrett, Ben, Adam and Elliot, and each of their wives were crowding around him. His baby sister Jessi and her husband Lash, his cousin Luke and his wife, Jasmine, were all there. So were Selene's three sisters and her two brothers-in-law. All told, they had eighteen more searchers than they'd had before. More important than that, though, was that they had family. There wasn't much you couldn't get done when family banded together.

"We can't have all these people milling around out here," Mick Flyte called. "Have them go into the nearest town and wait for word, Wes. We'll call them as soon as—"

"Sorry, Flyte. I don't work for you. And neither does my family." Wes spoke slowly, turning, keeping one arm around his wife's waist.

Flyte lifted his brows, looking around at all the people. "This is all...family?"

"Yep, aside from the few we left home watching the young'uns."

Garrett spoke next. "I realize it's unusual, Mr. Flyte, but in this family, when one of us gets into trouble, the rest come together to get them out of it. It's worked pretty well for us, and besides, once we make up our minds, we're not easily swayed.'' Then he turned to Wes. ''What's the latest?''

''I have a feeling they're west of here,'' Wes said.

Selene spoke then, her voice soft, her eyes betraying the shock and surprise of seeing them all here. It moved her nearly to tears, Wes saw that clearly. ''There was a radio call just a little while ago. While you were…busy, Wes. It was Alex, we think, calling from a helicopter. He could only give a couple of landmarks before…well, before he lost contact. He said there was a red butte, and a dry riverbed.''

Jessi Brand shouldered her way between two Federal Agents who were studying a topographical map of the area and she bent over it. Then she looked at the sky, then at the map again. Finally she straightened. ''The closest thing to what he describes is that way. About…'' She glanced at the men on either side of her.

One of them quickly looked at where her finger was on the map. ''About a hundred miles.''

''A hundred miles,'' Jessi repeated. ''Due west.''

''Let's go.''

And without waiting for permission from anyone, they all started piling back into the vehicles that had brought them. They had four SUVs and an oversize pickup with four ATVs in the extra-long bed. Gun racks in each vehicle were full up, even to the small ones on the rear of each of the four-wheelers.

''How the hell did you get those weapons onboard a commercial airliner?'' Mick Flyte asked.

''Didn't,'' Garrett said. ''Fortunately, I'm friends with a lot of Texas Rangers. And most of the Texas Rangers I know have plenty of guns. You know, of their own. Generous fellows, those Rangers. Always willing to share.'' He touched the brim of his hat, opened the tailgate of the pickup, pulled out two ramps and positioned them. Then he climbed into the pickup bed and got on the first of the four-wheelers, started it up and carefully backed it down out of the truck. Wes did the same with the second one. Luke took the third, and Ben the fourth.

Adam got behind the wheel of one of the SUVs with Kirsten, Penny and Kara piling in with him. Jessi and Lash jumped into the front seat of another, with Maya, Caleb and Jasmine taking the rear. The third SUV took off with Elliot at the wheel, Esmeralda, Edie and Wade riding shotgun. Chelsea jumped into the driver's seat of the pickup, and Taylor got in beside her, with Selene close behind.

They all took off into the desert, four all-terrain vehicles, three SUVs and a pickup truck bounding away like the cavalry.

Mick Flyte was left behind with his troops and his maps, shaking his head. He pounded a fist on the closest Jeep and said, ''Well, what the hell are you waiting for? Let's get out there!''

Twenty-five miles out, Wes ground the four-wheeler he was riding to a stop as he saw two forms staggering toward him across the desert. His heart leaping in his chest as he exchanged a glance with his brothers on either side of him, he gunned the thing into motion again, shooting forward.

''Mel!'' The pickup stopped, its door slammed, and Selene went running, shouting her sister's name. ''Mel, honey, are you all right?''

She stopped, though, before she got to her sister.

The other vehicles stopped, one by one, engines idling or shutting down. Wes stopped his beside his cousin Selene, who was just standing still, staring at the couple moving ever closer. "What is it, Selene?"

She didn't take her eyes off the bedraggled pair. "It's not her. It's not Mel. And that's not Alex, either."

Frowning hard, Wes looked again, squinting this time. "Oh, hell, it must be those other two." He battled the burning disappointment, told himself that if the two foreign dignitaries could survive, Alex and Mel surely could, as well.

"Everyone," he called, "these are the people Mel and Alex were impersonating. Katerina and Thomas Barde."

By now the two had made their way to them. The woman sank to the ground, her legs folding beneath her, while the man remained standing, weakly. His face was bruised, and he was obviously dehydrated. "Please, can you help us?" he asked.

Military vehicles came rolling over the ground behind the line of Brands. "Of course we can," Wes said. "But I imagine the men behind us are going to insist that's their department. They've spent a lot of effort searching for you. What can you tell me about the others?"

"Others?"

"The two who look like you. Alex Stone and Melusine Brand?"

Thomas Barde lowered his head, shook it slowly. "They insisted we take the parachutes," he said slowly. "They knew the chopper was going down, but they insisted...."

"No," Selene whispered. By then her sisters, Kara, Maya and Edie, were all around her.

"I'm sorry," the man said. "They were true heroes, both of them."

Kara began to cry softly, turning into Edie's arms,

while Maya only stared unblinkingly. "Mamma won't survive this," she muttered.

Selene shook her head. "Stop it. They're not dead. They're not. This man doesn't know anything for sure." She speared the man with her eyes. "Do you?"

"Well, I—"

"Did you see the chopper go down?"

"No. Alex intended to take it as far from where we jumped as possible, to lead our pursuers the wrong way."

"Which way?"

Frowning, the man pointed. By then the military vehicles were stopping. Mick Flyte was running forward, eager to take custody of the missing VIPs. Selene looked at her sisters. "Get back in the vehicles. We're going to find them."

No one argued, and a moment later the little convoy was speeding across the desert once again.

Chapter 13

"What do you suppose Curnyn is up to?" Mel asked.

She stood in the center of the room they'd been shoved into, looking around with wide, curious eyes. Alex rubbed his wrists, noting the red marks on hers. The guards had taken the cuffs off them, pushed them through the open door, then slammed and locked it.

This cell wasn't much different from their earlier one, except that it included crude furnishings. A wobbly card table and two folding chairs stood in one corner, with a kerosene lantern and a book of matches in the center of the table. Alex moved forward, levered up the glass globe and struck a match. When he touched the flame to the wick, flame blazed high and spewed black smoke, but he quickly turned the knob, adjusting the wick. When he lowered the globe into place, a soft yellow light spread through the small square room.

A rough blanket, folded neatly, sat on the floor in the

corner opposite the table and chairs. There were no windows, and the door that had been closed and locked was solid. There was no barred opening in the top, as there had been in the other cell.

"They didn't even leave the handcuffs on," Mel muttered as she walked around the room, running her hands along the walls as if in search of some secret exit.

She wouldn't find one, Alex knew. The floor was concrete, the walls cinder block. The ceiling consisted of barn beams, four feet apart, with floorboards nailed in the opposite direction across the tops of them.

Alex took it all in and got an inkling what was behind all this, but he couldn't be sure. He was damned if he wanted to tell her, though. But it looked to him like the noble offering of a last meal to the condemned. He glanced again at the blanket in the corner and wondered just what else their captors expected them to do for the last time before dawn came.

"Alex? What's the table for?"

As it turned out, he didn't have to lie to her, or struggle for a pretty way to phrase the truth. Before he could find the words to do either, there was a tap on the door. It swung open a beat later, quickly enough so he knew the knock had been just for show. An armed soldier entered, his rifle in his hands, and he was followed by another. As the two stood just inside the door, flanking the entrance, a smaller man walked in between them, carrying a heavy tray. He set it on the table, which rocked dangerously.

"What is this," Mel asked.

"It's a matter of honor." At the sound of Curnyn's voice, Alex and Mel both turned to see him standing at the doorway. "It's customary to feed the condemned a last meal," he said, looking toward them but never quite meeting Mel's eyes, Alex noted. He *really* didn't want to kill her, did he? In fact, Alex thought the man admired her, maybe even had a small crush. "Especially when the condemned are as worthy as the two of you. I'm afraid this is the best we could do under the circumstances."

"And how do we know it's not drugged just to keep us quiet until dawn?" Alex asked.

Curnyn nodded. "I expected you to think of that." Stepping into the room, he walked up to the rickety table, lifted the lid off the plate of food and took a fork from the tray, then scooped up a soggy bite of what looked like chicken stew. He ate it, then broke off a piece of the accompanying biscuit and popped it into his mouth, as well.

Alex nodded at the tin pitcher of water. "A little drink to wash that down, Curnyn?"

"Of course." Curnyn poured some of the water from the pitcher into a tin cup, and drank it down. Then he held the cup upside down to demonstrate that it was empty. "Perfectly safe," he assured them. "You will not die hungry or thirsty. If you wish for more, call the guards." Licking his lips, he glanced at Mel. "You have four hours until dawn. And then you will die a martyr. Your people will never forget you, Katerina. And even though history is, as they say, written by the victors, I will see to it that your true valor and spirit are recorded for all time."

"That'll be a great comfort while I'm being shot between the eyes, Curnyn."

He lowered his gaze. Alex didn't even bother watching the men leave. He was busy watching Mel, because her bravado faded as soon as Curnyn took his guards and left them alone. She stared at the door as it closed, and very slowly the horror of the situation seemed to paint itself over her face in white. She blinked, seemed to try to shake it off. But he saw the way her pupils contracted as if to shut out the light of realization. He didn't think anyone else would have seen any of it. But he was completely tuned in to her. He felt what she felt, and he knew what she felt right then, even before the locks turned audibly and she turned to face him and finally put the rush of emotion into words.

"My God, they really intend to kill us."

"Intentions are a dime a dozen, Mel. They don't mean a damn thing until they're carried out."

"But they will be carried out." She stared at him, her eyes hard, cold. "In four hours. Four hours. It doesn't seem possible that I might have only four more hours to be alive." She frowned then, her gaze lowering, turning inward. "I wonder if I'll feel it when the bullets hit me? I mean, will I die instantly, or…"

"Don't do this, Mel." He gripped her shoulders, squeezed them gently. "Don't let them mess with your head that way. I have no intention of just letting them shoot us, and I know damn well you don't, either."

"Well what do you suggest we do about it? We're locked in here, there's no way out, we're outnumbered and we're unarmed. They're going to come in here in four hours and march us outside and shoot us." She stared into his eyes, her own showing signs of panic.

"We're not dead yet, so don't start thinking as if it's over. It's not. It's far from over. Say it, Mel."

"It's not over." She drew a deep breath, closed her eyes. "It's not over. God, it can't be over."

He pulled her closer, hugged her to his chest. "I swear to you, it's not."

She nodded against him, and he felt dampness soaking through his shirt. Tears. She would hate like hell for him to know she was crying. "You're right," she said. "As long as we're still alive, there has to be a chance."

"There is."

"We might still be able to get out of this mess alive."

"We are *definitely* going to get out of this mess alive."

She sniffed a little, drawing one hand up to knuckle the tears from her cheeks, and tried not to let him see what she was doing. Then she finally lifted her head and looked up at him. "You're a great liar, Alex. Thanks for that."

"I'm usually a great liar. Hell, I'm *supposed* to be a great liar. It's part of my job description. However, that doesn't seem to matter with you."

"No?"

"No. You have this uncanny knack for seeing right through me. I've never met anyone before who could cut through all my bull, straight to the truth, as easily as you can."

"I can?"

He nodded. "I'm serious about this. Look at me, and you'll know I'm telling the truth. I really believe we have a fighting chance to survive this." She didn't quite look convinced, so he went on. "We have a code, you know. In the Secret Service. You can lie to anyone about anything if it's to protect the client. But no matter what else happens, you never, *ever* lie to your partner."

Her head tipped slowly to one side.

"You've been my partner from day one in this, Mel. You've watched my back, you've taken my crap, and you've never once let me down, no matter how scary things got. You could have left me a half dozen times by now, but you didn't. You stuck with me. I trust you more than any partner I've ever worked with. And I respect you too much to lie to you.''

She'd been staring into his eyes, her own swimming with emotions throughout his entire little speech, but at the end she suddenly turned away.

"Hell, I wasn't trying to make it worse," he said, sliding his hands over her shoulders.

"Well then, stop being so damn mushy. If you make me cry in front of you, I'll be forced to kick your butt."

"Sorry. I meant it, though. All of it."

"Yeah, right. Okay. And just so you know...me, too."

"You too? I give you a five minute declaration of loyalty, and all I get is a 'me too'?"

She drew a deep, nasal breath, straightened her spine and turned toward him again, but instead of looking at him, she looked past him, then walked past him to examine the food on the table. "I'm hungry, despite all that's going on. You suppose the food's safe?"

He had been expecting more. Hell, didn't she realize this could be their last night on earth? Maybe he'd done *too* good a job of convincing her they would survive this. Maybe that was because he honestly believed it. Hell, he had to believe it. He couldn't begin to even consider the possibility that he might lose her now. Not now that—

"Bleck," she said, examining the food.

Sighing, slightly disappointed that she hadn't thrown herself into his arms, he looked at the food, too. It wasn't much. Vegetables and chunks of chicken swimming in gravy. It looked like the kind you could buy dehydrated. Just add water. There were the biscuits, and the pitcher of water. "I don't think it's poisoned or drugged. But it looks a long way from safe."

"Oh, yeah, listen to the snob. You probably prefer gourmet cuisine." She was teasing him, getting a little bit of her spirit back. He was glad to see it.

"Actually, compared to this, I'd prefer fast food."

"Don't knock fast food. It's the most efficient source of empty calories in the Western world." She used the unused fork to spear a bit of gravy-moistened biscuit, drew it to her nose and sniffed. Then she grimaced. "Unfortunately, I think you're right. This chicken smells a little…off."

"What makes you so sure it's chicken?"

She tossed the fork down. Then she paused, stared at it and picked it up again. "Why do you suppose Curnyn cares if we eat it or not? Enough to take a bite himself just to prove it's safe, I mean?"

Alex lifted his brows. "I don't know. Actually, I think the man may have developed a crush on you."

"Oh, come on, Alex, I'm being serious here."

"So am I." Then he shrugged. "Hell, he's only human. I suppose there's no sense disappointing him." He took the cloth that had covered the tray when the man carried it in and spread it open. Then he scraped the food into it, bundled it up, set it in the darkest corner of the cell.

"What about the water?"

Alex looked at the water, sniffed it, even tasted a little on his fingertip. "I don't know. Curnyn drank it. I watched him closely. He definitely drank, he wasn't putting us on. But, uh…it could give you some stomach issues."

"I'm so thirsty I could drink from a mud puddle," she said. "And Mamma says I have a stomach made of cast iron. I think I can handle a little questionable water.'' She took the remaining tin cup, the one the other man hadn't touched, and filled it with water from the pitcher.

"Mel, I wouldn't do that," Alex warned, but he was too slow. She took a sip. Then she licked her lips and looked up at him.

"It's fine. Sweet, and even cold."

"I don't think bacteria have a taste."

She drank down the rest, then handed the cup to Alex. "It's fine. Have some."

Alex filled the cup, took a sip, just to see if he could detect anything. The water didn't taste off in any way. He resisted drinking it, though, just in case. He needed to be at 100 percent if they were to have any hope of escape. Getting sicker than hell from tainted water wouldn't do either of them any good.

"Now," Mel said, "let's see if any of this stuff can be used to our advantage." She picked up the forks, wiped them off and put them into her pockets. She lifted a tin plate. "If only we could sharpen the edges, we could fling it like a Frisbee and behead the bastards."

"I don't think that's gonna happen." Alex left her to rummage through the dishes, while he made his way around the cell's four walls, feeling them with his hands, just as she had done earlier. He pressed each block to see if anything gave. He checked the floor, as well, and then the low ceiling, but it seemed to be solid.

"I wish I had a nail file," Mel said. She was sitting in one of the chairs now, studying an empty tin cup. "They're as good as little daggers, you know."

"No, I didn't know that."

"Oh, yeah. My sister Edie would never be caught dead without a nail file. Neither would the princess, I'll bet. Pretty little princess. If she were the one locked up with you right now, she would have a nail file. Not that she'd know what to do with the damn thing. Besides filing her nails, I mean.''

Alex frowned. ''You're right, she wouldn't have a clue.''

''Come to think of it, there were lots of things in old Bernadette's makeup case that kinda looked like implements of torture. I didn't know what most of them were, but now I'm wondering if I ought to change my ways. Get my own makeup kit, you know?''

''You hate makeup.''

''Yeah.'' She laughed. Actually, she giggled.

Alex went utterly still.

''High heels. I should've kept the high heels. I could have driven one of those stilettos right between Curnyn's beady little eyes.'' Another giggle. High-pitched and totally un-Mel-like. ''Besides, they were sexy as hell.''

Alex crossed the room in three strides and knelt in front of her, his hands on her upper arms as he studied her face. Her head was a bit wobbly, and her eyes were all pupil. They could have swallowed him whole. She was smiling crookedly at him.

''If I were a woman like the princess, or Bernadette, I'd know all about all that stuff,'' she told him. ''I'd gut those bastards with my eyebrow tweezers, and I'd hot-wax their faces off and save us all.'' Her head lowered, hanging limply. ''But I'm not. I'm not. I'm a poor excuse for a female, and I know it.''

''The water was drugged. Dammit, Mel.'' He got to his feet, picking her up on the way, and he carried her to the corner where the blanket was. As he struggled to unfold and spread the thing with one hand, she looped her arms around his neck and nuzzled his cheek.

"I wish I were more like that whiny little princess."

"Why the hell would you wish a thing like that?" he asked, finally getting the blanket straight and dropping to one knee to lower her onto it.

"Because then you would want me the way you wanted me when I was being her."

He paused, bent over her, her arms still linked at the back of his neck, her face only a few inches away. "I've never wanted Katerina. Never even met her until today, and I didn't like her much. And I never wanted you because you were acting like her, or pretending to be her."

She blinked and tipped her head to one side. "Then it was the shoes. It was those sexy shoes, wasn't it? I could get used to them, I guess—"

He would have laughed if he hadn't been so damned worried. Was it lethal, what they'd fed her? Or just a tranquilizer? "It had nothing to do with the shoes."

"But you kissed me and…you know…you wanted to…"

"And you pick now to want to know why?" He sighed, shaking his head. She'd shot him down every time he'd even come near the subject.

She blinked, looking confused and a little stupefied, mostly due to the drug, but maybe a little bit by him. "Yes. I pick now. Tell me why. Why did you kiss me the way you did? If it wasn't the shoes and it wasn't Katerina…" She shook her head slowly, searching his face with unfocused eyes.

"Lie still now. We don't want this stuff working through your bloodstream any faster than it has to."

"Was it the clothes?" she asked, sitting up.

"No." He eased her back down, trying to keep her still.

"The hair? Was it the hair?"

"Mel, I wouldn't care if you were bald. Will you just lie still and be quiet?"

"Not until you tell me why!" she insisted, sitting up yet again.

"All right, I'll tell you why, but only if you promise to lie still."

She nodded very slowly, leaning back against the wall.

"I kissed you because I wanted to. Period. I wanted to kiss you, Melusine Brand, and I didn't care about your hair or makeup or shoes, or about much of anything else except how it would feel to kiss you. So I did."

He was kneeling beside her, leaning over her, hands on her shoulders trying to keep her from moving around too much. He started to move away from her, now that she was lying fairly still. But he got caught in her eyes and felt their pull, and knew he was way too close to her right now.

"Then…kiss me again," she whispered to him.

He licked his lips. "Not a good idea," he said. "Not now." But his heart wasn't in it. His gaze was on her mouth now, and he was craving it.

"It's our last night on the planet, Alex. If not now, then when?"

She lifted her head a little. He could have backed away, but he didn't. He let her press her lips to his, and then he wrapped his arms around her and kissed her some more. God, it felt good to hold her like this. He'd been spending his waking moments in doubt, his sleeping moments in need. But when he was touching her, kissing her, all those things faded away, and there was only this sense of rightness left. She fitted him like a hand in a glove, and all the 1001 differences between them didn't matter in the least.

He lifted his head, gently took his arms from around her and sat down beside her, leaning back against the wall, trying to digest the insane notions cycloning through his mind.

Mel slid herself across his lap, linking her arms around his neck and resting her head on his chest. When her lips nuzzled his neck, he closed his eyes in sweet agony. And then she whispered, "Make love to me, Alex."

He clenched his jaw as the blade of self-deprivation speared him. He held her gently, his fingers running through her hair. "You don't know how badly I'd like to take you up on that offer right now, Mel."

She looked stricken. "Then do it."

"I will. Don't you doubt it." He ran his palm over her face, cupping it, turning it up to his. "But when I do, you're not going to be half in the bag from some drugged H_2O, Melusine Brand. I want you at 100 percent. Aware, and completely involved."

She blinked, long, slow brush strokes of her lashes, trying valiantly to clear her unfocused eyes. "But if we die in the morning—"

"Are you telling me you think there is still even so much as a speck of a chance that I'm going to let that happen?" He shook his head. "Maybe before that invitation, Mel, but not now. Now I've got too much to look forward to."

She laughed, and it was loud, and a little drunk; then she curled into his arms and kissed him again. Her palms pressed to either side of his face, and she went to work on his mouth as if there really were no tomorrow. Every bit the aggressor, she explored with her tongue and tasted and suckled, and he relished every second of it.

Then she released his lips, lowered her head to his chest and went to sleep. Alex sat with his back against the wall, holding her cradled against him, her head on his shoulder, her arms locked around his waist. He stroked her hair, her skin, listened to her breathe. He didn't think the water had been laced with anything deadly. Thank God, he thought. If he lost her now...but, no, if it were dangerous, she would be showing signs of trouble by now. It was probably just supposed to keep them relaxed and complacent—to reduce the chances they would fight for their lives or plot another escape. Clearly, Curnyn knew they wouldn't give up easily. He knew they would fight to the bitter end, and Alex had no intention of disappointing the man.

But until he was ready, he thought, maybe it would be best to let Curnyn and his men think they had both imbibed the drugged water.

Chelsea was driving the SUV across the wasteland, so it was Selene who answered the cell phone when it rang.

"This is Mick Flyte," the voice on the other end said. "I need to speak with Wes or Garrett Brand."

Selene looked through the windshield at the cloud of dust and dirt illuminated by the SUV's headlights. Beyond that cloud, the two men were riding ATVs over rough terrain at speeds that, quite frankly, scared the hell out of her. "This is Selene Brand, Mr. Flyte. Neither Wes nor Garrett is available right now," she said. "But you can talk to me. I'll pass the message along."

There was a sigh. "Tell them I think I know where they need to go. There's an old government storage facility. It wasn't on the map, God only knows why. Used to be used to store government surplus stuff back in the fifties, but it's been abandoned since seventy-two."

"Where is it, exactly?" As she asked, she cradled the tiny phone between her ear and shoulder, and unfolded the topographical map on the seat. Mick Flyte spoke carefully, giving directions, and as he did, she traced the route from landmark to landmark with her finger. Finally she whispered, "My God, that's so far. We'll be lucky to make it there by daylight."

"You'd better," Flyte said. "We've intercepted some of their communications. They made the mistake of using cell phones."

"And?" Selene was almost afraid to ask.

"The radicals believe they have the real couple. And from what we've overheard, they, um…they plan to execute them by firing squad at dawn."

Selene blinked slowly. "Oh, my God."

"What? What is it?" Chelsea asked.

"Then I suggest you find some way to meet their demands, Mr. Flyte. If my sister is executed at dawn, I can pretty much promise you, there will be hell to pay."

"Executed?" Chelsea repeated.

"Executed?" Taylor asked, wide eyed.

Selene covered up the mouthpiece. "Flyte says that's what the lousy thugs plan to do. Shoot them at dawn."

Taylor turned to exchange a look with Chelsea. It was grim but determined. Then she faced Selene again. "We aren't gonna let that happen, hon."

Selene nodded, but turned her focus back to the man on the phone.

"There are no demands, Selene. Not yet," he said

slowly. "And even if there were, the government of Tantilla has its princess back, so they have very little interest in this matter. From here on, this is a U.S. operation. We're not going to get any help from anyone. To them Alex and Melusine are just a pair of strangers."

"A pair of strangers who saved their precious princess's life," she snapped as fury worthy of her sister Mel rose up and heated her blood.

"I know. Selene, believe me when I tell you that it wouldn't matter if the demands were met or not. They're going to kill them either way. The fact that they are acting so soon tells us that much. Mel and Alex are just too much trouble to keep alive."

"Bluff them, Mr. Flyte. Find some way to contact them and promise them anything they want. Just stall things, just a little. We'll get there in time. We will." She clicked the disconnect, set the phone down, looked at Taylor and Chelsea. "We need to go faster. Head toward this." She pointed to a canyon that showed on the map.

"Southwest from here. But it's dark. Dammit, I can't be sure we're going in the right direction," Chelsea said.

"There's a dried-up riverbed here somewhere. If we find that and follow it, it'll take us almost to them. But we have to hurry, Chelsea. We have to hurry."

Chelsea nodded, stomped the accelerator and pulled up beside the men on the four-wheelers, then she flashed her lights to get their attention and signaled them to follow her.

Chapter 14

She woke feeling groggy and hung over but warm. Of course she was warm; she was wrapped up tight in Alex's arms.

She lifted her head, stared up into his eyes, and saw in them a heat, a longing, right there in plain view. It was a look she had never seen quite so clearly in his eyes before. Oh, she had thought she might have glimpsed hints of it a few times, but never so clearly. There was no attempt to hide it, or disguise it, or even tone it down. He looked at her as if he could barely keep himself from ravaging her, right then and there.

What the hell had brought about this change?

"You're awake," he said, stroking her hair away from her face. "How do you feel?"

She frowned, taking careful stock. "My head hurts, and my mouth is so dry I could drink a gallon of wa-water...."

Water. Oh, God, she'd drunk the water, and it had

been drugged, and she had been loopy. She remembered Alex carrying her across the cell, sitting down with her. But then what had happened?

She closed her eyes, searching her mind.

She remembered kissing him. Kissing him in a way that made the word *kiss* seem like a dramatic under-statement. Had she really been sitting on his lap licking at his mouth as if it were the filling of an Oreo cookie?

But it got worse as her memory gradually came back to her. She remembered it all now. She had asked him to make love to her.

Worse yet, he hadn't complied.

She swallowed hard and couldn't quite look him in the eye as his coarsely spoken, throaty reply played it-self in her mind. She could hear it, and she could see the look in his eyes and feel the hardness of him.

I will. Don't you doubt it.

Her stomach knotted, and her entire body warmed at the memory. But had he meant it? she wondered. Or had he just been trying to humor her so she would lie still and recover?

She got out of the intimate embrace in which the two of them had apparently spent the past few hours. She got to her feet, hugging her outer arms and rubbing them against the sudden chill as she paced away from him across the cell.

"Listen, they'll be coming for us any minute. We don't have a hell of a lot of time to talk about this, Mel, so it has to be now. Are you awake? Is your head clear enough so you're going to retain any of this?"

He wanted…to talk about it? She closed her eyes, her back to him, and her heart beat a little faster. They had only moments left to live, maybe, and all Alex had on his mind was talking to her about what had happened between them last night. And making sure she would understand him and retain what he told her. Maybe he really had meant what he'd said to her last night. And maybe there was more that he still hadn't said but felt he had to tell her now.

"My suspicion is that the food and the water were both laced with that drug, whatever it was," he said.

She turned around slowly, blinking at him. "B-but Curnyn ate some. And he tasted the water, too. You were sure he did."

"The drug could have been in the cup. He drank from the other one. As for the food, I don't know, there might have been a bite pushed off to one side. He scooped it up so fast I couldn't really see if he got it from the main pile or not. Could you?"

"No. I guess not."

Alex got to his feet, too. "And if that's the case, it would have been enough to keep us out of it for hours. We need to let them think we downed every bit of it. That way they won't be expecting us to try anything."

She nodded slowly, looking at the floor for a long moment before finally lifting her gaze to his. "So that's what you want to talk about before they get here to take us to our execution? A plan?"

He frowned at her. He didn't say it, but she heard it clearly screaming from the deep furrows between his brows. *What the hell else would I want to talk about?*

"If they try to tie your hands, hold them like this." He clenched his fists, pressing them together. "Have your wrists crossed, but angling in opposite directions. Keep as much space between them as you can without being obvious. Here, try it."

She put her wrists out in front of her, her lips pressed tight, as she mimicked his demonstration. For some reason it was very easy to remember to clench her hands into fists right now.

Alex put his hands around her wrists, pressing them together. "Resist, but try not to let me know you're resisting. Hold them as far apart as you can, but make it look like they're touching."

She did it, and he nodded. "Good. That's good."

"Thanks."

"They'll probably stand us up against a wall," he went on, talking fast, pacing the room, not even looking at her. "When they start shooting, hit the dirt, then scramble right at them. That's gonna throw them off more than anything else. They would expect us to run, not attack. That moment of surprise could save our lives. All right?"

"*That's* the plan? Run toward them as they shoot at us?"

He lowered his head. "And turn down the blind-fold."

She shook her head. She'd been in doubt before, but now she was certain his reasons for turning her down last night had been totally bogus. There was no way in hell they were going to live to mate another day.

"How about we just beat their brains in when they come for us, take their guns and shoot our way out of here?"

The door opened. Six armed men marched through, two by two. The leader came in last. "It is time. Come along."

Mel started forward, but Alex grabbed her and yanked her into his arms, holding her passionately against him. Even as she returned the embrace, nearly limp with relief, he whispered near her ear, "Remember to act as if we're still drugged."

Even that, the final embrace, was just part of the plan. She nodded and pushed him away. Then she let her body slouch a bit, sniffled once, then twice, and faked a very nice, whiny-voiced, "I don't wanna die...." drawing out the final word and making lots of crying, sobbing sounds.

"Awww, come on, honey, they aren't really gonna shoot us. Guys, come on, tell her," Alex attempted. "It's all just a joke, right? Right?"

"Bind them!" Curnyn said.

The nearest young soldier slung his gun over his shoulder and pulled a pair of handcuffs from his pockets. He strode forward, pulling Alex from the wall, turning him around and pulling his hands behind him.

"Curnyn, please!" Mel cried.

Curnyn held up a hand to stop the other men from moving. "What is it, Katerina? Anything I can do to make this less painful for you, I will gladly comply."

"Don't handcuff us."

He lowered his head, pursed his lips. "You must be bound. You're too clever to leave free."

"Then tie us with cloth or rope." She held her wrists out. "The cuffs have rubbed my wrists raw."

Curnyn rubbed his chin, then nodded. "So be it. Bind their hands with rope."

One man scurried from the room and returned with lengths of what looked like twine. One guard twisted the rope around and around Alex's wrists, pulling it tight and hard, knotting it firmly.

God, it looked tight. He came to her next. She turned around, made her hands into fists and wept more loudly than before. She craned her neck to look over her shoulder at him, begged and pleaded with him, howled in his ears, and all the while kept all the pressure she could on the rope as he twisted it around her wrists and finally knotted it off. He hurried, probably to get away from all her wailing. She thought her wrists were probably much less tightly bound than Alex's were. In fact, as soon as she turned back around, she relaxed her hands, pressed her wrists as close together as she could and felt the slack in the rope. My God, Alex was right. She was going to be able to get out of it.

But when? And what the hell was she supposed to do once she did?

"Come," Curnyn said, his voice firm. "We go now." Men pointed weapons at Alex and Mel, and they were marched side by side across the room, through the doorway, into the hall. Mel kept up her pretense of weeping, and Alex staggered drunkenly. Up a flight of stairs and out into the blaze-orange light of a tequila sunrise. She didn't know when the dawn had seemed more beautiful. And she didn't know if she would ever see another.

The soldiers marched them to a cinder block wall that seemed to have been part of an unfinished building. Its highest point was just below Mel's shoulder blades.

They were stood against it. Then the soldiers marched away.

A troop of men marched into position ten feet in front of them.

"Alex, we're not gonna make it," she whispered. "My God, look at them all."

"Get your wrists free. Hold on to the rope so they don't see it."

She obeyed, wriggling her hands out of the knots easily. "But, Alex, I—"

The leader came toward them, lifting a blindfold toward Alex. He turned his head away. "No. No blindfold. None for my wife, either. She will die with courage.''

Nodding, the man stepped away.

''Alex, I can't die without telling you—''

''Mel, listen to me. What I have to say now is very important. I want you to forget about what I said before and just remember this.''

She thought she knew. She thought she knew what he had to tell her. Finally. God, finally, now that they were only a heartbeat away from dying.

''Yes, Alex? Tell me.''

Curnyn shouted ''Ready,'' and the soldiers brought up their weapons.

''Go over the wall, Mel.''

''I love you, too,'' she blurted, and only then realized what he had said.

''Aim!''

''Over the wall,'' he repeated. ''Now!''

She spun around, hands pressed to the wall at chest level, and she launched herself over the top, landing hard on the other side as the man shouted, ''Fire,'' and bullets peppered the cinder blocks.

''Alex!'' She thought for one horrible moment that he hadn't made it over. But he was there only a split second behind her. He gripped her arms, pulling her up and into motion. The soldiers gave chase, leaping the wall, running around it, firing at them.

They ran behind one of the outermost buildings, pausing breathlessly to look back. ''Oh, God, there's nowhere to go!'' Mel cried. ''They're coming! They're coming, Alex.''

''They're coming from this way, too,'' Alex said, peering around the other side of the building. Then he said, ''Wait a minute. What the hell is that?''

Mel peeked around her corner again. The soldiers had all stopped racing toward them and were now looking back the way they had come. Then Mel heard what had caused them all to turn away. It was a sound, like…a roar. Like motors growling ever closer. And suddenly there were vehicles skidding into sight from a cloud of dust, people climbing off them and out of them, then scurrying for cover even while shouldering weapons. They began firing at Curnyn's men without even a second's hesitation.

Men fell to the dirt, wounded and howling, while Curnyn shouted orders to return fire. Other men fell without a sound and never moved again. Some returned fire, while others ran for cover. But the distance was too far. They were out in the open, and the Brands were coming closer now, marching in line, a wall of blazing fire and the smoke of gunpowder. Soldiers started throwing their weapons down and putting their hands up, while those few who had managed to get a safe distance away made a run for it.

"My God, look! It's the family!" Mel felt warm all over. Her smile must have damn near split her face. "They came for us."

"Damned if they didn't," Alex said. "Will you look at them? Even Edie and Kara—"

"Are they out of their minds? They gave *Kara* a loaded weapon?"

The firing stopped. The Brand men rounded up those who had surrendered and herded them into the nearest building, then locked it up, while the others kept a careful watch around them for snipers. Selene, the only one without a weapon, called their names.

"We're here," Mel called. She took Alex's hand, and they stepped out from behind the building. "We're okay. God, I'm so glad to see you.'' Mel released Alex's hand and opened her arms, trying very hard not to break down into a blubbering mass of teary relief.

Selene raced toward her, crying openly, but suddenly Mel saw her little sister go chalk-white and stock-still, even before she sensed the presence at her own back. His hand slid around her neck, and a gun barrel pressed to her head. ''If anyone moves, she's dead.''

Curnyn. The bastard had been hiding in the very building she and Alex had ducked behind for cover. Alex stood beside her, stiff and poker-faced.

Selene backed up slowly, holding up her hands, muttering words Mel either couldn't hear or couldn't understand. They sounded foreign.

The man placed a hand at the flat of Alex's back and shoved him forward, and Alex stumbled a few steps before stopping himself.

''Get over there with the others,'' he ordered Alex. ''Now!''

Alex walked a few more steps toward the Brands, but not too far. He stayed very close, right between Mel and her family, facing them.

''The rest of you drop your weapons,'' Curnyn said.

When they were slow to comply, he worked the action of the gun he held to Mel's head. She could feel his hands shaking, wondered just how sensitive the trigger was, felt fear creeping through her.

''You don't want to do this, Curnyn. This isn't honorable. Killing me for the sake of your cause and your people is one thing. But this isn't the same. You're using me to save your own life.''

''Shut up. These people know you. They called you Mel. You've deceived me all along. You're not Katerina.''

"You got that right," Alex muttered, turning to face them. "She's ten times the woman Katerina is."

She met Alex's eyes, and they were intense. They held her gaze and burned their message into her brain. She swore she knew what he was thinking. Oh, sure, she thought. She hadn't been right about what Alex Stone had been thinking yet. Why would she start now?

He shifted his gaze to the ground, then up to her, to the ground again, then up to her. Then his brows rose just a little.

She moved her head downward, a very slight nod. She thought she understood.

Alex seemed coiled, ready to spring. It was all up to her. God, did she have the courage to pull this off?

"All I want is safe passage out of here," Curnyn told Alex. "Across the border will be fine. I'll let this one go when I get there. But if anyone tries to stop me, I promise you, she dies."

"Do you have any idea how sick I am of hearing that lame old threat?" Mel asked. "I mean, for God's sake, Curnyn, if you're gonna kill me, just do it already."

She drew her elbow back hard and fast into his solar plexus. The sudden pain and surprise made Curnyn loosen his grip on her neck, and she threw herself bodily to the ground. She hit hard, and it knocked the wind right out of her. The moment she hit the earth, Alex was lunging at the bastard, leaping on him like a pit bull.

Curnyn's gun went off as the two men went to the ground, rolling in the dirt, struggling for the weapon. It dropped from between them, and Mel scrambled to pick it up. Garrett and Wes were there instantly, pulling the two apart, wrestling the leader to his feet. Garrett handcuffed him and shoved him up against the nearest building.

Alex was on the ground, breathing hard, and Mel rushed to him, gripping his arm and helping him to his feet. "Are you okay?"

He got up slowly, brushing the dust from his knees, thighs, the front of his shirt. Then he paused, looking down and blinking slowly. "Well, I'll be damned."

Mel looked down—and her heart seemed to skip a beat when she saw the red stain spreading on the front of Alex's shirt.

"Bastard shot me," Alex said, lifting his bewildered gaze to her.

"Alex?"

He dropped to his knees.

Mel dropped, too, gripping his shoulders. "God, he's been shot! Alex! Alex, please." She ripped his shirt open, but she could see only blood. It coated his chest, slick and shiny, and more seemed to be pulsing from the darkest spot, in the center.

He fell over backward, and she went with him, but his eyes were closed and his body limp. "Somebody do something!" Mel shouted.

"There's a chopper on the way," Garrett said, pocketing the radio he'd been using. "Ben? Wes?"

Ben and Wes were already crouching beside Alex, spreading the shirt open. Ben said, "Chelsea, take care of Mel."

"It's okay, hon, just let 'em be," Chelsea said, tugging Mel out of the way.

"No. God, no." Mel let herself be pulled away, but only a few steps. "Not after all this. I can't lose him. I can't."

"Selene, get down here. We need you," Wes snapped. To Mel he said, "Just give us some room, hon.

We'll try to keep the bleeding in check until help gets here.''

Selene knelt with them, as the others backed off to give them room. Mel didn't know what the hell was going on. But she trusted them. She trusted her sister, too. She didn't back away very far, just far enough. Selene held pressure on the wound, closed her eyes, muttered to herself. Ben and Wes held their hands over hers, and they muttered, too. At first it seemed a garbled bunch of gibberish, all of them saying something different, none of which Mel could understand, but then it seemed to gel and settle into one mantra, which they repeated over and over, their voices taking on a melodic drone and falling into perfect rhythm. The words sounded Native American. And for a moment Mel swore there was a glow emanating from the three sets of hands pressed together in the center of Alex Stone's chest. It was as if a soft white light glowed from that spot. But that couldn't have been real, and it wasn't. It vanished as soon as the clouds shifted position over the sun. Just an optical illusion.

She heard the reassuring propeller beat then, looked up and spotted the helicopter on the horizon. ''They're coming,'' she said. ''They're almost here. And look, the rest of the cavalry is right behind them.'' She saw jeeps and other vehicles bounding closer, too. ''You're going to be okay, Alex. You have to be okay.''

''Must be Mick Flyte and the government men,'' Garrett observed.

Ben and Wes and Selene just kept on chanting.

Alex wasn't sure what had happened. His head felt odd, and he had no idea where he was or how long he'd been there. His throat hurt. His chest hurt. In fact, as feeling returned very gradually to his body, he realized that pretty much everything hurt. The only part of him that felt good was his hand, because it was held in a warm, firm, blessedly familiar one.

He pried his eyes open but saw only light and shadow, out-of-focus shapes with blurred edges.

"Alex?"

"Mel?" He squinted at her until she came clearer. But before he could focus, another image came to mind, very clearly. The one of Curnyn holding a gun to her head. His heart almost stopped when he saw that image, and he sat up fast, reaching toward her. "Let her go, you son of a—"

He froze in racking pain, one hand going automatically to his chest as Mel leaped to her feet and grabbed his shoulders.

"It's okay, Alex. It's okay. Curnyn's behind bars, and I'm fine. Just take it easy. Easy now, everything's all right."

There were bandages on his chest where his hand was. He realized it dully as Mel eased him back down onto the pillows. She pulled the blanket up around him and fussed over the tubes that were taped to his arm.

"Are you...were you hurt?" he asked her. He tried to see her, to look her over to determine for himself that she was unharmed, but his vision was still unfocused, and he couldn't be sure.

"No, dummy. You were. That would be why you're the one lying in the hospital bed and I'm the one sitting vigil, instead of the other way around." She shook her head. "Some cloak-and-dagger type you are."

He almost laughed, but it turned into a grimace. Still, the pain began to ebb as he relaxed in the bed. His vision cleared, and he looked at her, standing over him.

She was all cleaned up, her hair freshly washed and lustrous. She was wearing jeans and a cute little T-shirt that hugged her in all the right places. The front read Fear This. He smiled a little, and then he noticed that her blue eyes were moist, and more than a little bit droopy. "You've really been sitting vigil?"

"Sitting vigil, standing vigil, pacing vigil. You probably didn't know it was possible to pace vigil, but I've proven it over the last several hours."

"You didn't sleep," he said, stating the obvious.

She only shook her head. "Look, just so we're clear on this, I'm assuming that you wouldn't have slept if it had been me with the bullet in my chest and the surgery and the recovery and all that other nonsense. I mean, you would have paced vigil, too. Right?"

"Surgery, huh?" he asked.

"I'm sorry, Alex. I didn't think… Yeah, they had to do surgery on you, to get the bullet out." She reached down to the floor beside her and picked up a small glass jar with a misshapen gray lump of lead inside it, and shook it around so it jangled. "But I made them save it for you. See? Isn't it cool?"

He looked at the bullet, felt a jab in his chest at the sight of it, and nodded. "Very cool. But, uh, a little off the subject." He took the jar from her and set it beside him on the bed. "You wanted to know if I'd have done the same for you."

"Would you?"

Her eyes held his like magnets, and he knew just what she was asking. "Yeah," he said. "I'd have paced a hole in the floor."

Her lips pulled at the corners just a little. "I thought so. But…you know, I wasn't sure."

"No? Well, that's easily explained. I mean, you said you loved me, and I never said it back."

She blinked. "I didn't—I never—"

"Sure you did. Remember, when we were standing in front of the firing squad, and I said, 'go over the wall,' and you said, 'I love you, too'?"

She pressed her lips tightly. "I kinda thought you might have forgotten about that."

"Well, I didn't. And I'm sorry I didn't give the appropriate response to such a heartfelt declaration, but things got a little crazy just then."

She shrugged. "Well, actually, you did."

"I did what?"

"Give the appropriate response," she said.

Alex frowned at her. "I did?"

She shrugged with one shoulder. "Sure you did. I mean, you muttered it enough times when you were coming out of the anesthesia. Most of the nurses on the staff of the hospital heard it several times over. They told me, of course, but they wouldn't let me in there to hear it for myself."

He had the oddest feeling. He'd had it for a long time now. A sense of completeness. As if he'd found some part of himself that had been missing. "No one's pointing any guns at us right now, Mel. And you're not drugged, and I'm not under the influence of anesthesia. And you know what?"

She met his eyes. "What?"

"I still love you."

Her smile grew wider. "I know."

"Well?" He took her wrist and pulled her closer to him. "Don't you think you ought to say something back to me?"

"Oh. You mean you don't already know?"

He shook his head from side to side.

"But I thought I made pretty clear to you, in the cell, after I drank the water."

"I'd like to hear it from you when you're straight and sober, if you don't mind."

"I said it again, when we were about to be shot."

"I'd like to hear you say it without a gun to your head."

She smiled fully, every bit of mischief he loved so much twinkling in her eyes. "I love you, Alex." She said it, and then she leaned in closer, pressing her lips gently to his. "I love you way more than I think I should."

"Why?"

She sighed, stroking his hair and looking into his eyes. "Well, look at us. I can't come to you in your world, Alex. I can't. I don't fit in, and even if I could, I wouldn't want to. I don't like it there."

"I wouldn't want you to like it there, Mel, and I sure as hell wouldn't want you to fit into that world. That would mean changing, and I don't want anything about you to change. I love you for who you are. That's the woman I want to be with."

"Really?" She smiled a little. "Are you sure?"

"How can you ask me that at this point? We're meant for each other, Mel, haven't you figured that out yet?"

She nodded. "I can't imagine any other man being good enough."

"I don't care where we call home," he told her. "Just as long as we're there together. And…you don't mind traveling when we have to."

"I don't mind traveling. But why would we have to?"

"Well, you know, it's essential in the private security business. If you're going to be my partner, you'll have to—"

"I'm gonna be your partner?"

He licked his lips. "In every possible way I can think of." He said it with a smile, and then he kissed her again. "There's no one I trust more, no one more capable, and to be honest, I've never met anyone who seems to thrive on being shot at quite as much as you do."

She rubbed her cheek across his face. "Yeah, well, at least I know enough to get out from in front of the bullets."

He laughed, and it hurt. "I promise I'll try to do better."

She lowered her eyes. "You got shot trying to protect me."

"I just wanted to keep you healthy for the wedding."

She lifted her eyebrows.

"I know, it's a pretty pathetic proposal. To tell you the truth, I wanted to wait."

"For what?"

"Oh, to do it right. I was gonna rent a limo to take you to a fancy place for dinner."

"Or borrow a horse and ride down to the swimming hole for a picnic."

He smiled. "I was thinking of hiding a great big ring in the bottom of your glass of champagne."

"Or maybe in the bottom of a beer bottle." She snuggled closer. "Take note, I did not object to the 'big ring' part."

"Then I was gonna get down on one knee," he told her, "and take your hand and tell you that I couldn't live without you, and ask you to be my wife."

"So why did you decide to do it here instead?"

He shrugged. "I can't wait to hear the answer, I guess. I need to know if I'm going to get to spend the rest of my life in bliss with the only woman I've ever loved."

"You are," she told him. She bent down and kissed him, aggressively, the way she'd kissed him in the cell that night. And when she lifted her head away, he was breathing hard. "You lucky son of a gun," she whispered.

"Hey, baby?"

"Hmm?"

"Get the doc in here, would you?"

"Why? Are you okay?"

"Yeah. I just, uh, have a few questions about how soon I can return to…normal activity."

Her smile was slow and knowing as she leaned down to kiss him again.

*   *   *   *   *

*Turn the page for an
exclusive excerpt from*

EMBRACE THE TWILIGHT,

the newest **WINGS IN THE NIGHT** *novel
from Maggie Shayne,
coming in March 2003 from Mira Books.*

1

A hand clasped him by his hair and jerked his head up out of the tub of frigid water. Will dragged in a desperate, hungry breath, before that hand shoved his head into the tub again, holding him under.

His hands were bound together behind his back, his legs bound at the ankles. His body screamed with pain, but all that dulled beside the stabbing need in his lungs as they spasmed in search of air. Small red explosions danced behind his tightly closed eyes. He was going to pass out, and then he would drown.

The hand jerked him out of the water again, and even as Will sucked in greedy, noisy breaths, slammed him down into a small, ladder-back chair.

A bearded man wearing a spotless white headdress lifted Will's chin and stared down at him, then spoke to one of the guards.

''He has returned to his body. You may resume the torture now.''

''Why should we waste our time? He will only leave again when the pain becomes too much for him. How does he do it? Where does he go?''

The first man shrugged, crossing the floor of the cave to where a fire had been burning earlier. It was now a bed of glowing coals. They'd placed long iron rods in the embers, and it was one of these the man pulled out.

"Now, Colonel Stone," the man said, speaking heavily accented English. "You will tell me what I wish to know."

"I've told you already," he said softly, though it hurt like hell to talk, because of his split, swollen lips and the dryness of his throat. "There are no American spies in your training camps."

There were, actually. There were thirteen, and Will knew who they were, what names they were using and what camps they had infiltrated. They would have received word of his capture by now. They would remember their training, and they would know exactly what to do, where to go, when to meet there for extraction. It would take them another forty-eight hours to get out of harm's way, he thought. Judging the passage of time was tricky, given the circumstances.

He had to hold on until the men were safely out of the country.

"If there are no spies, then how do the Americans always seem to know our plans?"

The man laid the cherry-red end of the iron flat across Will's chest. The pain was beyond bearing, and he tipped his head back and grated his teeth against it.

Even when the rod was lifted away, the pain remained. He closed his eyes, tried to find that place inside his mind where he'd been hiding before. That place where the pain couldn't reach him. He saw the woman, standing far in the distant reaches of his subconscious. Sarafina, the dark, exotic fantasy woman who lived out her tales in his mind so vividly that she swept him away from the torture, the pain.

He'd stumbled upon her quite by accident, when they had beaten him nearly unconscious. He'd been hovering on the edge of oblivion when he'd seen her in his mind's eye. Just her eyes, glowing black eyes. He found himself focusing on those eyes, getting caught in them, sinking slowly into their black-water depths, into darkness. He'd felt himself sinking deeper, and as he did, the pain vanished. Once it fell away behind him, he emerged on the other side, in some other place and time, as a silent, invisible observer of the woman's life.

Ever since that first time, he'd found he could use the pain to find that place again. The trick was to just give himself over to the agony, not to fight it, but to embrace it. And then he would close his eyes and search for hers. All he had to do was find her eyes, stare into them, and he would sink again into her world, where the pain couldn't reach him.

She was pure fantasy, as was her story. He knew that. But she was also his salvation. And the salvation of those thirteen Americans who would be tortured to death unless he kept their names secret.

So he closed his eyes as they placed the hot brands on his skin. He relaxed his jaw and tried not to fight the pain. He let the pain drive him closer to her, closer, until she turned and faced him. Her eyes opened wide as he fixed his upon them and rushed willingly into their cool black depths. Then he was completely immersed, having left his body far, far behind. He swam, every stroke taking him farther. And he wondered if one of these times his captors would do him the favor of simply killing him, so that he could remain in that other place. But would it remain, opening, welcoming him inside? His own custom-imagined heaven? Or would it vanish as his brain cells slowly died?

At this point he wasn't certain he cared.

Silhouette Books
**is delighted to present
two powerful men, each of whom is
used to having everything**

On His Terms

Robert Duncan in
LOVING EVANGELINE
by *New York Times* bestselling author
Linda Howard

and

Dr. Luke Trahern in
ONE MORE CHANCE
an original story by
Allison Leigh

Available this February wherever Silhouette books are sold.

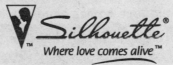

Where love comes alive™

New York Times bestselling author

DEBBIE MACOMBER

weaves emotional tales of love and longing.

Here is the first
of her celebrated
NAVY series!

NAVY *Wife*

Dare Lindy risk her heart
on a man whose duty
would keep taking
him away from her?

*Available this February
wherever Silhouette books
are sold.*

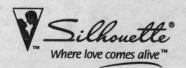

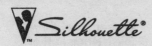

COMING NEXT MONTH